I0760551

QUEENS OF THE FAE
BOOK TWO

FAE'S DEFIANCE

MELISSA A. CRAVEN
& M. LYNN

Edited by Cindy Ray Hale
Proofread by Caitlin Haines
Cover by Maria Spada

For our families, who make all the insanity of this job so much easier.

PRISON REALM
NORTHERN VATLAN
LOCH VILLANDI
FARGELSI KINGDOM
SOUTHERN VATLA
DRAGUR FOREST
VINDUR CITY

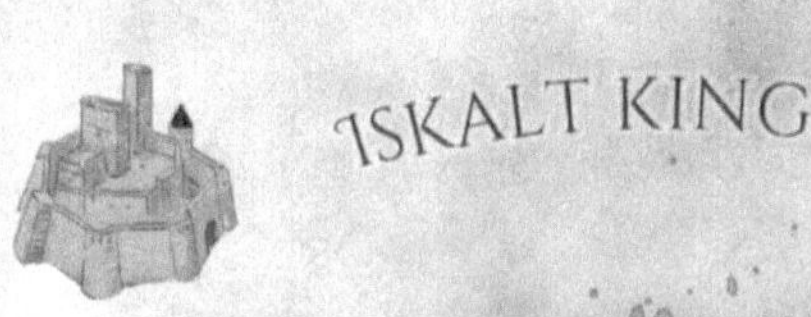

ISKALT KINGDOM

EASTERN VATLANDS

ELDFAL

SANDUR

SOL LOCH

DUR KINGDOM

TEOTANN OASIS

ELDUR DESERT

CH LANGT

RADUR CITY

Prologue

Alona

Alona Cahill trudged along the river's edge, eager to leave her prison cell behind for a brief taste of fresh air. The chains around her ankles chaffed, but they were better than the bars of her cage. After surviving the last weeks in the dungeons of Queen Regan's palace, she looked forward to this part of her routine.

Every week, the prisoners were escorted from the dungeon to get some fresh air and exercise in the fields beside the river. It was the only time she was able to wash the filth and grime from her body. And the only time she had to speak privately with Neeve, her fellow prisoner and co-conspirator.

"How is it coming with the chains?" Alona asked her friend.

"It's slow work. My magic is nearly useless, but every day

the links grow weaker. I'll be able to start working on yours soon." They had little hope of escape, but that didn't mean either woman was ready to give up trying.

Alona was born without magic and therefore no help in terms of the power, but she had other skills. Since she was thrown into her cell, she'd worked tirelessly developing relationships with each of the guards. She knew which ones were susceptible to her charms and which ones weren't worth the effort. She knew their shifts, when they ate, when they slept, and when they weren't paying attention.

A few were a lost cause while others had a soft spot for the helpless little princess. They sometimes brought her extra food or water, which she shared with Neeve in the cell beside hers. In time, she hoped she could count on one of them looking the other way when she and Neeve made their escape.

The girls sat soaking their feet in the river, talking softly of their plans, using the rush of the water to conceal their voices.

"You're too obvious." A fair-haired man in chains sat down beside them, eying Neeve curiously. "You may as well shout your plans across the field." He eased his blistered feet into the water, breathing a sigh of relief.

"I don't know what you mean," Alona said sweetly.

"If you've found yourselves imprisoned in the lowest, darkest corners of the dungeons, it means one thing. You've angered the queen, and she will not soon forget it."

Neeve looked away, and Alona couldn't help feel sorry for her—well, she felt sorry for all of them. Everyone in the dungeons had heard of the girl executed for helping someone escape the palace. Moira, her name was. Neeve had barely been able to speak of her except to whisper her name in her sleep. Alona didn't know how, but they'd known each other.

She shifted her attention to the man before them. His eyes spoke of immense grief, but his calm façade hid it well. "You've been here a long time, haven't you?"

"Longer than you've been alive, Princess."

"You know who I am?"

"I know exactly who you are, Alona Cahill, daughter of the Eldur queens."

"If you know my mothers, then you must know I won't give up until I find a way out of this prison."

"If there was a way out, I would have found it long ago."

"Who are you, sir?" Neeve asked. Even as a prisoner she couldn't seem to drop the formality a life in service had instilled in her.

"Brandon O'Rourke." He held his hand out to her.

"You're the queen's brother?" Neeve's eyes widened with shock as she took his offered hand. "The rightful king of Fargelsi?"

"Please, call me Brandon." He held onto Neeve's hand longer than most handshakes lasted before releasing it quickly.

"You're supposed to be dead," Alona whispered.

Brandon's shoulder slumped as he swirled his aching feet in the soft mud of the riverbed. "I may as well be."

"Time to go, you three," the queen's guard called.

Alona groaned as she got to her feet, dreading the return to her cramped cell.

"Be more careful, ladies. The queen has eyes and ears everywhere."

Alona and Neeve made their way along the river's edge and back into the tunnels that led behind the falls and into the bowels of the palace dungeons.

"Get in your cages, and be quick about it," the guard called, shoving prisoners along the well-worn path.

Alona stepped inside her cell, noting the fresh layer of hay that would make her bed for the next week or more. Hers was a bit thicker than the others. Smiling at the guard, she sank to her knees, pulling her tattered blanket around her shoulders. The warmth of the afternoon outside left her quickly as the chill of the dungeon seeped into her bones.

"What's happening?" A frantic voice bounced off the stone walls. Another new prisoner trying to resist what was happening to him. "This is a mistake. I'm a nobody." The guards shoved the boy through the gates where he fell, sprawled across the floor in a tangle of long limbs and strange clothes.

"Seriously? Dude, that wasn't necessary." The boy stood up, glancing around the room in the dim torchlight. "I definitely didn't do anything to deserve this. Where am I?"

"Shut up, human." The guard guided the boy to the empty cell beside Alona's.

"Human?" Neeve murmured, clutching the bars of her cell. "He talks like Brea."

"Brea?" The boy's eyes snapped to Neeve's.

"Where is she? Is she here? Brea!" The boy shouted, earning a blow to his head from the guard's club.

"Du-ude." He rubbed the lump on his head. "We need to get you some anger management classes. Not cool, bro, not cool."

"Get inside and shut up." The guard opened the cell door.

"I don't think so." He shook his head, taking a step back. "I'm going to need a bigger cell. I have an issue with tight spaces."

The guard shoved him inside and slammed the door closed.

"What's his problem?" The boy rubbed the top of his head, leaning back against the cold stone wall.

"Quiet. You'll only make it worse on yourself," Neeve whispered. "How do you know Brea?"

Alona leaned closer, wanting, *needing* his answer.

"How do *you* know Brea?" He turned his wide eyes on Neeve.

"I served her."

The boy stared at her. "Served her? Is she here?"

Neeve's grin was grim. "Not anymore. She escaped."

"Who are you?" Alona asked.

"Myles Merrick, best friend of Brea Robinson who I'm guessing is a lot more important in this world than the one we came from."

Why did everyone in this fracking fae world lie?

Brea still couldn't believe the fantasy life she'd fallen into. Okay, more like been dragged into kicking and screaming. She shook her head to rid it of thoughts that would inevitably lead back to the biggest liar of them all. The man who'd claimed she was the subject of a prophecy. Prophecy-schmophesy. It didn't exist.

Her hands tightened around the steaming cup on the table in front of her as she focused on this moment's lie. "And what do you call it?" She looked to the bear of a man sweeping the floor with an ancient bristly broom that looked like it belonged in a bedraggled Cinderella's hands instead of this giant. Did giants exist in Eldur? Maybe he was a half giant—like Hagrid.

"What?" She hadn't heard the answer he gave her.

"Girl." The man she'd come to know as Xander over the last few weeks leaned the broom against the stone wall and rounded the small wooden tables separating them. He folded himself into a chair that was entirely too small for him. "I wouldn't begin to guess what a girl like you was doing spending every day out here in the city without an escort."

"A girl like me?" She grimaced. "What does that mean?"

"A richie." Adamina singsonged as she bounced from the kitchen at the back of the small tavern. At this early hour, Brea was their only patron.

"Hey, Mina." Brea gave her a little wave.

Mina set a bowl of sugared oats in front of Brea and another before her father.

Brea took a bite, savoring the simple fare that was a world away from the more robust foods of the palace. "How do you know I'm a..."

"Richie?" Mina crossed her arms over her petite frame. She looked nothing like her larger father. Brea had learned weeks ago that it was just the two of them. Mina's mother died in childbirth. "It's the clothes. You won't find cloth as fine as yours here in the city except on the backs of nobles. Tell us, Brea, which family do you belong to? Is it the Wilsons? They've always been so secretive, though Viscount Wilson gets pretty chatty in here over his cups."

Brea shook her head.

Mina's eyes lit up, and she flicked them to the cup in front of Brea. "Oh, it's the Robinsons, isn't it?"

Brea almost spat oats across the table. How did they know?

Mina kept talking. "The Robinson clan is the wealthiest in the city."

Oh. Brea released a breath. There was a clan of that name in the fae world.

"That's why you enjoy Eldur beans so much. They control the Eldur bean trade."

"Eldur beans?" Brea stared down into the dark molten heaven in her cup. The lie she'd forgotten everyone seemed to be in on. "I was told there wasn't such a thing as coffee."

"I don't know what coffee is, but even as a Robinson clan member, you wouldn't drink Eldur bean brew." She leaned in, dropping her voice. "It's a commoner's drink." Her nose wrinkled. "But if you ask me, it's much better than the tea all you richies drink."

"Adamina," Xander chastised. "That is enough. I don't smell the day's bread baking in the kitchen yet."

She held her hands in front of her chest. "I know. I know." She shot Brea a wink. "We won't tell your brothers of your taste for Eldur brew when they come in seeking ale this evening." She bounced away, her bright red hair flowing out behind her.

Xander scrubbed a hand across his face and leaned back in his chair. Now that Mina pointed it out, Brea could see the differences in how these people dressed. Instead of the colorful silks and soft linens used for clothing at the palace, they adorned themselves in worn woolen tunics with no hint of color.

"Please forgive Mina for her intrusiveness."

Brea shrugged. "I'd be curious about me too." She drained the rest of her Eldur brew. "Am I really not supposed to be drinking this stuff?"

Xander eyed her, his gaze shrewd. "If you were really of the Robinson clan, you'd know the expectations of society. Brea, you are not much older than my own daughter, and I like you."

"Um... thanks?"

"But you are here every morning by yourself. Women of an obvious higher station are targets in this part of the city and must be careful."

Brea tried to see the city as he did. In truth, she loved traversing the streets and wandering through markets full of life. It took her mind from the fact that Lochlan and Finn had been gone for three weeks without so much as a word.

Xander sighed. "Do you not have people worried about you?"

She thought of the woman she'd recently learned was her mother, but Queen Faolan had no time for her when the real people she cared about were gone.

Queen Tierney tried, but there was only so much kindness a person could take before they broke. Well, if that person was her.

"Do you want the truth, Xander?"

He nodded.

"Okay." She sucked in a breath, preparing herself. "I was a prisoner in Fargelsi for weeks. The queen wouldn't let me leave, forcing me to escape through the swampy Vatlands where I came face to face with creatures I couldn't even begin to describe. Finally, I reached Captain O'Shea's camp and saved them all from a terrible fate." A little fib never hurt anyone. "I had to fend off enemies from Iskalt and protect the soldiers, eventually taking a sword to the shoulder. It hurt, but not as much as letting the Captain suffer." She released a fake sob.

Xander stared at her, his mouth dropping open as she continued to sniffle.

"I knew it!" Mina's squeal came from the kitchen doorway. "We all heard about the girl who escaped Fargelsi, and then you turn up, a stranger in our city."

"But you thought I was a Robinson."

She laughed, the sound holding a musical quality. "I've known the Robinsons since I was a child. They are frequent visitors to the tavern. You don't carry their ghastly looks." She giggled behind her hand. "I just wanted to pull the truth out of you."

Xander looked from Brea to Mina. "I didn't hear of an escaped prisoner."

"That's because you never leave this box of a tavern, papa." She plunked herself down across from Brea. "Did you really save Lochlan?" She sighed. "Have you seen his eyes when his magic rises? They're like an icy spear straight to my heart."

Xander scowled. "Mina, that is the queen's man."

Ignoring Xander, Brea leaned across the table toward Mina. "Did you know he reads?"

Mina fanned her face. "Oh my."

Brea laughed at the younger girl, enjoying the lightness of the moment. Usually when she thought of Lochlan, it was with a mixture of annoyance and worry. It felt good to chat with Mina as if she were just a friend. Maybe she could be.

Xander pushed his chair back and stood. "Guess I'm making the bread," he grumbled.

Mina ignored him. "So, you live at the palace?"

"Only because they don't know what to do with me." Half-truths. That wasn't the reason she was there, but it didn't change how little she fit in those gilded halls with people who rarely smiled.

At least when Griff was lying to her, he made her feel like she belonged.

After telling Mina all about what the palace was truly like, Brea looked up to find patrons walking through the front door looking for their lunch.

"Crap, I've been here all morning." She jumped to her feet.

Mina stood. "Papa is going to be angry with me, but I do hope we see you tomorrow, Brea."

Brea nodded. In truth, she couldn't wait. The city and this tavern kept her heart beating when it wanted to freeze in her chest. With a wave goodbye, Brea stepped out onto the busy street. Sandstone buildings rose up before her, each more boring than the next. It wasn't the mundane architecture of the lower city that breathed life into everything around her, it was the people.

A cart rumbled past, and she jumped out of the way

before following the crowd to the market square where people sold their wares. Everything from fresh fruit to home-spun clothing and ceramic dishes.

A butcher slammed a slab of meat onto a table near her, making her jump and clutch her chest. She watched him hack away at it with a cleaver before moving on. One booth caught her eyes. A handmade sign read Eldur beans. She wondered if she could get someone at the palace to make some Eldur brew from them.

Fishing a few gold coins Tierney gave her from her pocket, she approached the vender.

A young man, probably only a few years older than her met her gaze, sliding it down to take in her clothing. "You're the one who escaped Fargelsi."

How did he know?

As if sensing her question, he smiled, revealing a wide gap between his two front teeth. "We recognize strangers here."

"Oh." She held out two coins, and his eyes widened.

"Do you even know how much money that is?"

She shook her head.

"Enough for this here whole cart of Eldur beans and then some. It's only two coppers per bag, but I'mma give you one for free." He smiled again, satisfied with himself. "Anyone who defies Regan of Gelsi is a friend of Ollie's." Ollie must be him.

"You don't have to do that."

"Sure I do, miss—"

"Brea."

He nodded as he reached for a canvas sack and scooped Eldur beans into it. "All right, Brea. Though, with you living at the palace, I dunno what you want with Eldur beans." He handed her the bag.

"Thank you, Ollie."

His grin widened. "Hey, Lew," he called, looking toward one of the other carts. "A richie knows my name."

She really had to get some new clothes so everyone would stop calling her that. Her parents in Ohio had never been well-off. Compared to Myles' family, they were poor, and they dressed like it. Eyes followed her as she escaped from the market as fast as she could, uncomfortable with the attention.

If Lochlan were there, he'd bull his way through the crowd, leaving ample space for her in his wake. Finn would probably grab her elbow and make sure she was okay.

But they weren't there, leaving her alone once more.

Keeping a tight grip of the Eldur beans that would keep her sane in this place, she left the market behind, ducking into a familiar building on her right. Once inside the quiet bookstore, she released a breath and leaned against the door.

"Brea, that you, dear?"

"Fiona." Brea sighed in relief as she caught sight of the silver-haired woman walking toward her. She'd met the older woman at the palace when Fiona was tidying the library. The queen hired her to rotate the books and keep the selection fresh—with the exception of the human books. Those always stayed.

"Are you okay?" Concern etched into her every feature. "You look stressed."

She pushed away from the door. "I wonder why."

Fiona was one of the few people in the city who knew everything—well, almost everything. She didn't know Brea was the real daughter of Faolan.

"Still no word?" She set the book she was carrying on the front counter.

Brea shook her head. "Not so much as a messenger." She followed Fiona farther into the two-story store. At the back, a spiral staircase led to the upper stacks, a section Fiona called her human stories. Brea laughed the first time she found all the leather-bound tomes depicting stories about the human world.

She'd told Fiona the humans wrote about fae worlds as well, and they'd both had a good laugh at that. The first laughter Brea felt since learning the truth about her identity.

She was a changeling. Abandoned by her mother to be raised in the human realm where the things she saw and did because of her fae heritage made her an outcast, deemed a lunatic.

She still hadn't forgiven her mother for that.

And what about Alona? She grew up thinking she was one of the unfortunate fae born without powers, someone destined to join the serving class.

It wasn't fair to either of them.

"I know what you need, dear." Fiona led her up the back staircase. "I found a book I think you will enjoy greatly. It is meant for children, but..." She ran a finger over the spines until she came to a book of stories called *Humantales.* Just like the humans called them fairytales.

A smile spread Brea's lips as she flipped open the cover and thumbed through pages about princesses and kings that were obviously influenced by real human history.

Fiona put a hand on her shoulder. "Only a few fae clans have ever had the ability to open portals into the human realm, but over the centuries, many stories have filtered out and spawned fables of a world without magic."

"Why would anyone want stories about a world that didn't have magic?" She stopped on a page depicting Henry VIII as a benevolent king. It was a love story. She snorted. What would these people say if they knew the real history?

Fiona smiled softly. "We always want to imagine a world different than our own. Magic is not the great force some claim. It destroys just as much as it saves. Sometimes, I wonder if our world wouldn't be so broken without it."

"The human realm is broken too, Fiona. You don't need magic for that."

Fiona sighed. "The human world has wars and strife, yes, but magic has erased entire kingdoms from the fae world."

"What?" She snapped the book shut. "There was a fourth kingdom?"

"It serves only as a prison now." Sadness tinged her eyes. "Magic can sometimes be like dropping a nuclear bomb into a situation that calls for the delicate carving of a knife."

"Wait... how do you know about nukes?" Brea wracked her brain for anything that made sense. As far as she knew, the fae didn't have that technology. They didn't need it with their magic.

Fiona tapped her nose. "Follow me."

They walked down the stairs and crossed the store to the front counter. Fiona rounded it and reached into a compartment below, pulling free a book. She set it on the counter, and Brea's eyes widened.

"Where on earth did you get a US history book?" She ran a hand over the cover that showed a map of the country she'd called home most of her life.

"The palace library."

"You took one of Lochlan's books?" A smile slid across her face.

Fiona flipped through the pages. "He lets me borrow them as long as the queen doesn't find out. She only allows him to bring them back from the human realm if he agrees to keep them close. She does not want human books leaving her walls."

Brea understood immediately. If the people of Eldur read human books, they might make the connection to her. No one could know Lochlan travelled to the human realm.

"Fiona?"

"Yes?" She glanced up, her glasses perched on the end of her nose.

"You said only some families can create portals. How many are there now?"

"Well, that we know of in the last few decades... two. The Rifkin Clan is the nearest to the prison realm, though, so if travelers wish to pay them for passage, they must traverse those haunted lands. The Eldur courts do not recognize their noble status."

"And the other?" She already knew the answer.

"The O'Sheas." She smiled. "There was a time when they ruled Iskalt that the queen and king were great friends of ours. Eldur and Iskalt had an unbreakable bond."

She swallowed, barely able to breathe. "What happened to them?" She knew Griffin and Loch's parents died when they were boys. How old had Griff said he was? Two?

Fiona put the book away, a sad set to her shoulders. "They came to visit Queen Faolan. It was a grand visit with balls and banquets. When they left, the future looked so bright. I remember it as if it were yesterday. The rumor was they had a mission for Queen Faolan, but the queen and king of Iskalt never made it home."

"They died?" she whispered.

Fiona nodded. "Their bodies were found near the border of Fargelsi. Within months, the king's brother took the throne and sent Lochlan and Griff to be raised in foreign courts. Most people think it was a show of good faith to keep Eldur from attacking to reclaim the throne for Lochlan. But when her greatest friends died, our queen seemed to have lost her taste for war."

Tears hung in Brea's lashes. "I need to go."

Fiona called a goodbye, but Brea barely heard her as she rushed out in the blazing Eldur heat.

Sweat dripped into her eyes, but she kept going, barely registering that she'd left the Eldur beans behind. She clutched the humantale book under her arm and rushed through the busy streets, wishing she wasn't so far from the palace.

All she wanted to do was collapse onto her bed and hide in her room. Because she now knew without a doubt that Lochlan's parents were dead because of her.

"Lady Brea, rushing back to the palace already? It's hardly mid-day."

Brea paused at the sound of her name, blinking at the exotic woman dressed in free-flowing silks outside the magic shop. That's what Brea called it anyway.

"Mrs. Moran. I'm sorry, I've got to get back early."

"Come by later today. I have some new herbs to show you. They arrived today from the fire plains. I can teach you all about their mystical properties."

For a moment, Brea was tempted to join her. She was fascinated with Mrs. Moran's apothecary shop. Everything she stocked held magic of one kind or another. It wasn't the kind of magic she was supposed to be learning, but it was definitely more interesting considering Brea hadn't felt her magic in weeks. Something had her blocked, and she wasn't sure how to move past it. No one seemed too concerned about it so she went along with it.

"I'll try," Brea called over her shoulder.

"Go have a nap, dear, you look a bit peaky. And have a cup of that tea I gave you yesterday. It will help you rest."

"Thank you, Mrs. Moran." Brea picked up her pace. Some of her favorite shops were closer to the palace, but they knew her as Lady Brea there. She much preferred the anonymity she had at the marketplace across the river in the lower city. It was like a different world down there. The merchants in this part of the city catered to the nobility and wouldn't dream of calling her or anyone else a 'richie', at least not to her face.

By the time Brea reached the bridge entrance to the palace, sweat poured down her back, and she was anxious for a cool, quiet afternoon in her grotto. She might actually take that nap if her mind would quit running in an endless loop of worry and regret.

Shouts and commotion interrupted her thoughts. Sneaking into the courtyard wasn't going to work this time. Both queens and half the palace swarmed the entrance, shouting and issuing orders. Soldiers and horses stood by while a distinguished looking man gave a report to the queen.

"Brea, darling." Tierney spotted her before she could creep up the stairs. "There you are."

"I was just exploring some of the shops." She inched closer to the woman who called herself one of her mothers. "Have you had news of Alona?" Brea eyed the distraught

Queen Faolan, still unable to fathom her as the woman who gave birth to her. Both queens were wonderful people, but with Alona's disappearance and now no news from Lochlan and Finn, they were distracted. Most of Brea's interactions with her mothers were awkward in the extreme, none of them knowing quite how to act around each other. Brea tended to avoid them.

"We've had a disturbing report." Tierney put her arm around Brea. She was the more touchy-feely mom. "One of our scouts found the remnants of a battle. All of Lochlan's men were slaughtered."

Brea took in a sharp breath. "Loch and Finn too?" It surprised her how much it hurt to ask the question. Lochlan was a self-righteous pain in her butt and Finn was more of a stranger than a true friend—not like Myles had been. But that they both might be dead had her feeling all sorts of terror she hadn't expected. Like she couldn't possibly face this life in the fae realm without them.

"No, thank the heavens. There was no trace of them, so we must move forward hoping they made it to safety."

"But?" Brea braced for the bad news.

"It's been more than a week since the battle. Lochlan would have sent for help if he was able."

"So, they might not have made it?" She couldn't imagine Lochlan in any situation where he didn't come out on top.

"We can only hope news of their whereabouts will reach us soon." Tierney's eyes followed her wife's movements as Faolan issued orders. "But it is possible they've been taken back to Iskalt."

"His uncle will kill him." Brea's hand went to her throat.

"It's not likely Callum O'Shea would kill one of the last of his clan." Tierney squeezed her shoulder. "The O'Sheas have remarkable magic that is too precious to snuff out over something as petty as a throne."

Brea didn't think Callum O'Shea would agree with the Eldur Queen Consort.

"He is like a son to Faolan. To us both, really. He grew up right here with Alona."

"Lochlan is tough and resourceful. He can take care of himself and Finn." But Brea worried about Finn. If they got separated or were injured, would either of them have enough sense to come back home, or would they be stubborn and pigheaded and insist on looking for each other?

"Brea." Faolan gave her a curt nod as she approached. "Good. You're home. Do try to stay close to the palace, darling. We don't want to lose you too." Her words were kind and motherly, but she was utterly absent, just saying the things she thought she needed to say.

Awkward silence hung between them, and Brea just wanted to escape.

"Er—how will you look for them?" she asked.

"We've sent several scouts to scour the area surrounding the battle scene." Faolan stood, wringing her hands, refusing to look at Brea. She did that a lot. And sometimes when she did meet Brea's eyes, she could see the disappointment there. Disappointment that she wasn't Alona. "All we can do now is wait and hope they haven't fallen into Callum's hands."

"Please let me know as soon as you hear any news." Brea

stepped away from the queens, feeling the awkward much more than usual. "I'm just going back to my room now."

"We will see you at dinner." Tierney turned and led her wife back to the throne room.

Brea sighed as she retreated to her room. A warm breeze swept through the open hallway, and parrots chattered in the gardens. The Eldurian palace was so beautiful. She could get used to calling it home—if there was something here to hold onto. More than just pretty rooms, exotic gardens, and strangers for mothers.

But the one thing Brea would never get used to was how boring the life of a noblewoman was. In the human world, she had school to fill her days, therapy appointments, time with Myles, and Netflix. There was always something to do. In the magical realm of the fae, her days were filled with aimless wandering and endless, uncomfortable dinners with her mothers.

If that was the life of a princess, Brea didn't want any part of it.

"Brea?" Rowena called from her closet. "Is that you?"

"Yes." Brea sighed, closing the door behind her. She supposed it was too much to ask for an afternoon to herself. Rowena was a kind servant, but she wasn't Neeve.

"I was just seeing to some new dresses Queen Tierney ordered for you. There's a lovely new day dress that will match your eyes."

"I don't suppose you've managed to find me some comfortable pants and shirts?"

"A Lady doesn't need street clothes." Rowena

harrumphed as she fluffed a pillow to within an inch of its life.

"Good thing I'm not a lady." Brea collapsed on the couch in her sitting room.

"As long as you live in this palace you will dress and act like a lady."

"Maybe I should look for my own place." Brea got a kick out of riling up her maid.

"Lady Brea, your mo—the queen would not allow it." Rowena's cheeks flushed pink.

"What do you know?" Brea turned accusing eyes on the maid. No one other than the queens themselves and Lochlan —who might be dead—knew Brea was their true daughter.

"I know that this room is a mess." Rowena made to dust the spotless dresser.

"Spill it, Ro." Brea crossed the room.

"I was there." Rowena refused to meet her eyes.

"Where."

"The day you were born." Her eyes filled with tears. "Twas a happy day. For a time. Until the queen asked me to bring you to the Iskalt king." Rowena's bottom lip quivered.

"You switched us?" Brea sank down on the nearest chair.

"At the queen's order. Though I never understood why, I did as she asked. And I loved our dear Alona. Such a sweet child. And a good head on her shoulders, that one." Rowena polished the brass dresser knobs to a shine. "Always thought she and Lochlan would make a go of it one day. Knew he would raise her up from the serving class to be a proper lady if she couldn't be our princess." She dabbed at her eyes.

"And now here you are, come home to us at last. Just as ornery and full of mischief as Alona—in your own way. You could have been sisters, as alike as you are different."

"You were her lady's maid?"

"Of course. And I wouldn't hear of it, letting another care for you."

"Thank you." Brea pulled the fussy woman into a hug.

"For what, my Lady?" Rowena returned her hug with gusto, her arms a motherly embrace Brea had never known.

"For caring whether I'm here or not." Brea rested her head on Rowena's shoulder for a moment.

"Oh, sweet dearie." Rowena patted her back. "You listen to Rowena now." She held Brea at arm's length. "Your mothers rearranged the heavens to keep you and Alona safe. Give them some time. It can't be easy to gain one daughter only to lose the other. You're strangers now, but you won't always be. One day all four of you will be a family. And a strong one at that."

"We can hope." Brea forced a smile for the loyal servant.

"Go rest, my Lady." She swatted Brea with her dusting rag. "It's the hottest part of the day. No sense in trying to get anything done till it cools this evening."

Brea snorted. "Not that I have anything to do but stare at the walls anyway." She shed her lightweight overgown and retreated to the grotto for an afternoon nap. With nothing else to do, sleep was the only activity she looked forward to these days.

"Up with you, Lady Brea." Rowena pulled the blankets off the bed. "And don't give me any of your tantrums either."

Brea rolled over, clutching her pillow. "I don't throw tantrums," she muttered. "I simply protest the morning."

"The queen is bringing your breakfast herself. I suggest you get up and comb that rat's nest on your head." Rowena tossed a fluffed pillow on her head and went to make a ruckus in the closet.

"Which queen?" Brea yawned as she sat on the edge of her bed. What was the point of living in a palace if you couldn't sleep all day?

"*The queen* is always Faolan. We call her consort *Queen Tierney* to avoid confusion."

"Do I have time for a bath first?" Brea could use a cold shower to wake up, but the fae didn't believe in things like quick showers. At least not among the nobles. They believed a bath should be an event, something to enjoy—which she was all for, but a hot bath in the morning did nothing to wake Brea up.

"No. Now get dressed. She'll be here in a moment." Rowena tossed a blue day dress on her bed. She was a far cry from the triplets at the Gelsi palace. Or even Neeve.

"Yes ma'am." Brea stifled a smile for the gruff lady's maid. There wasn't anything Rowena wouldn't do for Brea, but at the same time she didn't treat her like she was made of glass. Of all the fae she'd met, Rowena had quickly become one of her favorites. Neeve was still her number one, though. She'd give anything to have her with her, not as a maid, but as a friend.

Brea dressed quickly and ran a comb through her hair.

"Do you know what she wants with me?" Brea walked into her sitting room, still brushing the tangles from her hair.

"Just a simple breakfast with my daughter." Faolan smiled from her seat at the small tea table in front of the balcony. "Please join me, darling."

"Oh." Brea forgot how to walk. Her mother made her nervous, especially when her other mother wasn't there as a buffer. She managed to set her comb on the table beside the settee and crossed the room to sit with the queen.

Too many queens in my life.

Brea swept her long hair over her shoulder. "Wait. Do I smell—?"

"I hear you enjoy Eldur Brew in the morning." Faolan poured a cup of the rich dark brew. "What do the humans call it?"

"Coffee." Brea inhaled the heavenly aroma. "Oh, this is even better than the kind they serve in the tavern."

"What was that?" Faolan poured herself a cup.

"Oh nothing. It's delicious, thank you."

"I'll share a secret with you." Faolan's eyes crinkled when she smiled—rare as it was. "The only reason I get out of bed most mornings is for a hot cup of Eldur Brew. It's popular among the commoners for a reason. I'm convinced it's the secret answer to all the world's problems."

"Your secret is safe with me as long as you share." Brea sipped from her cup, convinced her mother's fae coffee was better than the real thing.

"I owe you an apology." Faolan buttered her toast. "I

owe you a good many apologies. But this morning, I'm here to say I am so sorry I've been ... such a mess since your return."

"I understand." Brea took a slice of toast for herself. "You raised Alona as your own. I can't imagine how you must feel since she was taken."

"I miss her." Faolan's eyes misted with unshed tears. "But that is no reason for me to neglect you when you probably feel like a stranger in our home."

Brea didn't know what to say to that, so she shoved toast into her mouth to keep from saying something she might regret.

"It never occurred to me that you might be bored. But why wouldn't you be? We've given you nothing to do. No wonder you prefer exploring the city to sitting here in your rooms."

"It is kind of like watching paint dry." Brea focused on the selection of jams rather than meet her mother's eyes. She didn't bother to ask how Faolan knew how she spent her days in the city.

"Alona had tutors up until last year. Perhaps you would like a tutor to teach you all about Eldur and the fae world? We can arrange that for the coming months. Though you will soon need to focus all your energies on your magic when you come of age."

Brea nodded, her mouth full of toast she didn't taste. Clearly the Eldur queen intended Brea to make the palace her permanent home. She wasn't so sure she agreed with that.

"Lochlan once told me you grew up on a farm in a small village. He said you seemed to like the horses the most."

"We had horses when I was younger, but my father had to sell them after a few bad years and failed crops. My friend Myles lived on the farm next to ours. They always had horses."

"Did you know we have stables here at the palace? And not just for transportation purposes. We raise draft horses and ponies. Landowners from all over Eldur come to our stables for the best horses in all of the fae realm."

That piqued Brea's interest. "Where are the stables? I've explored all over the city and the palace grounds, but I haven't stumbled onto it."

"Behind the palace gardens at the top of the canyon. You may visit the stables whenever you like, but I thought you might like a job there as well."

"A job?" Brea's mouth hung open.

"Not that you need a job. You're not obligated by any means," Faolan rushed to add.

"When can I start? What will I be doing?"

"You can start today." Faolan smiled. "One of the guards will escort you there and back. You'll meet with Master Arturo, and if you'd like, you may apprentice with him."

"Apprentice? With the stable master? I just figured I'd be mucking out stalls."

"Master Arturo wouldn't dare ask you to do that." Faolan smiled. "He won't treat you any different than the other hands, but he will teach you horse breeding. He's a busy man, so he won't always have much time for you. While you're there, you'll exercise horses, watch over the pregnant mares, groom and feed the ponies. They always need extra attention."

"Sounds perfect." Brea couldn't wait to get started.

"I apprenticed under Master Arturo when I was your age. The stables are still my favorite place in the whole city. You get your love of horses and Eldur Brew from me." Faolan took her hand, giving it a gentle squeeze. "And your fair share of my awkwardness too."

"Awkward?" The queen didn't have an awkward bone in her body.

"Oh, I've learned to hide it behind cool smiles and a queenly facade I've perfected over the years, but inside, I'm still the girl who spills her tea and forgets how to articulate a sentence when I'm nervous. But I don't want to hide from my daughter."

"Thank you so much for the apprenticeship. I won't let you down."

"You couldn't if you tried, darling. Wherever your future leads, learning under Master Arturo will be good experience. As your mother, I want you to be happy and make your own decisions about how you fit into our family and our kingdom. I know I am not an easy woman to know, but I hope you'll give me ... us time to work our way into a real mother-daughter relationship. And when Alona returns, I do hope you can be friends."

"I like the sound of that." Brea squeezed her hand back. It was the most unawkward moment they'd shared since Brea arrived in Eldur.

"I leave you to your morning." Faolan cleared their breakfast dishes herself and retreated to the hall. "Oh." She turned just as Brea stepped behind her, and they collided, sending the breakfast tray sailing across the room.

"Oh, darn it." Faolan stooped to pick up the broken dishes.

"Like mother, like daughter." Brea laughed and went to retrieve the silver tray. They scrambled across the floor to clean up the mess. "I'm pretty sure Rowena would yell at us for daring to clean this up."

Faolan rocked back on her heels, laughter dancing in her eyes. "I'm pretty sure we did it wrong anyway." She stood brushing crumbs from her gown. "I was just going to tell you that you can find me in the throne room most days. You are welcome to visit us there anytime, Brea dear."

"I'll do that."

Faolan paused at the door for a second time. "Not a day went by during your whole life that I didn't think about you and wish good things for you." She didn't wait for a reply before she left Brea standing there with tears in her eyes.

"Finish grooming Raven, and you can call it a day, Lady Brea." Master Arturo slapped the fat pony on her ample rump. "Good work with the ponies this week. They're madly in love with you already."

"I think fae ponies are extra sweet." Brea brushed Raven's long fluffy mane until it sparkled in the sunlight.

"You spoil this one." Arturo chuckled.

"She's close to foaling. She deserves some extra attention." Brea smoothed her brush over Raven's back. "You think it'll be any day now?"

"Three or four more days yet."

"She looks ready to burst."

"I'm guessing this one is twins."

"Twins! Oh please send word as soon as she goes into labor. I want to be here with her."

"I'll send one of the boys to get you when the time comes, but I'm under strict orders to get you home before dark, so off you go, Lady Brea."

"Thank you, Master Arturo." Brea took her grooming tools back into the massive stables and went to wake her babysitter.

"Emmet." Brea shook the boy who was supposed to be her chaperone while she was working at the stables. He couldn't be more than fifteen, and she was pretty sure she could take him.

"Yes ma'am, Lady Brea." He scrambled to his feet. "You ready to leave, my Lady?"

"How many times have I told you to just call me Brea?"

"Yes, miss." Emmet trotted along behind her. She found it utterly ridiculous that she spent her days caring for horses, but when it came time to leave for the palace, she had to wait for Emmet's inept fumbling to saddle their horses for the ride back. He refused to let her help because 'a lady should never saddle her own horse.'

"I could walk there faster," Brea muttered, rolling her eyes when Emmet tried to give her a boost.

With her new job at the stables, Brea also had a new wardrobe much more to her liking. Today she wore tall black boots, comfortable trousers that could almost pass for leggings, and a linen tunic belted at the waist. With her long hair in a messy bun, she almost felt normal.

"Race you back to the palace." Brea mounted her horse and trotted across the stable yard.

"Lady Brea, I won't fall for that again. Please let me do my job and escort you home."

"Fine. But try not to ride like my eighty-year-old granny. I'd like to get home before I die of boredom."

Emmet's cheeks flushed. "I was always told when escorting a great lady I should travel at a comfortable pace so as not to tax her."

Brea snorted in a very unladylike way. "Well, I'm not a great lady, so that's your first mistake."

"Of course you are a lady, ma'am." He shook his head like he thought she might be crazy. She knew that look well.

"Well, I'm not made of glass. Do you have sisters, Emmet?"

"Four, my Lady."

"Then treat me like one of your sisters." She glanced back at him, but she'd made it worse. He looked utterly scandalized.

"I couldn't. It wouldn't be proper."

"Oh very well, Emmet. Ride ahead and make way for the Lady Brea." She waved him on like the grand marshal in a parade. There was no way this kid thought she wasn't weird.

They took the back roads to the palace. The queen insisted on it. She didn't want it to become common knowledge that a guest of the palace also worked in the stables as an apprentice. It was supposedly for Brea's own safety, but Brea thought it was more about keeping the whole switched daughter thing a secret.

Brea followed Emmet through the orchard. Large pods hung from the massive tree trunks. They looked a bit like coconuts, but the seed pods inside were more like Brazil nuts.

"Brea?" A familiar voice sounded from among the trees.

"Who's there?" Emmet put himself between her and the voice.

Brea threw her leg over the saddle and jumped to the ground. "Finn?" Her heart lurched into her throat at what she saw. "What happened?" She dropped beside him where Lochlan rested against a tree.

Finn sank down next to her, clearly exhausted.

"Talk to me, Finn." She moved to drape Lochlan's arm across her shoulders. He was injured and burning with fever.

"We were ambushed, and Loch was hurt bad. We've been trying to get home for days." Finn reached out to lean against the tree.

"Are you hurt?"

"No, but Loch needs help now. Take him and go. I'll just rest here." He sank to the ground in a faint.

"Emmet, help me get Loch on my horse." She heaved his weight, barely managing to get him to his feet. He groaned in protest. Emmet supported his other shoulder, and they moved him toward her horse. Loch's shirt hung in tatters around his lean frame and filthy bandages covered his middle.

They finally settled his dead weight across the saddle, and Brea climbed up behind him, careful of his injuries. "Get Finn and bring him back to the palace. I'm taking Lochlan ahead."

"No my Lady, you must wait for me."

"I'm not asking for permission." Brea reared her horse around and took off through the orchard toward the palace.

"Don't die on me, you stubborn fool." She held on to Lochlan tightly as she charged down the dirt path that led into the canyon and the palace courtyard. She normally went home through the rear palace entrance where the kitchens were, but she needed help getting Lochlan to the healers.

Flying over the cobblestones, she raced for the palace entrance. "I need help!" She called ahead, not prepared for the palace guard to stop her.

"Halt!" Several soldiers crossed their spears barring her entrance. "What business do you have at the palace?"

"I live here, you fool! Stand aside."

"Lady Brea," the soldier's tone changed. "I didn't recognize you without your finery."

"Let me pass. I have Lochlan O'Shea, and he's injured."

The guards rushed out of her way, ushering her inside the courtyard and calling for assistance.

Brea jumped off her horse and stood back out of the way while the guards carried Lochlan into the palace. "Take him to the healers now! You four, go look for Finn and Emmet. They shouldn't be too far from the orchard." She ran inside and headed straight for the throne room.

"Your Majesty!" she shouted. The guards moved to stop her, but she shoved past them. "Let me through. I found Lochlan." The guards stepped aside and opened the doors for her.

"Your Majesty!" Brea stumbled into the room. The rich plush carpet at her feet tripped her up and she fell.

"Brea?" Tierney and Faolan rushed to her side. "What's wrong?" They searched her over, looking for injuries. "Where is the blood coming from, darling?"

"Not my blood." She gasped. "It's Loch. He's back and injured. Finn was with him too."

Both queens left her on the floor and raced from the throne room. Brea glanced around at the line of commoners waiting to meet with the queens. Lords and Ladies sat in the balcony above, looking down their noses at her.

"I'll just be leaving now." She cast her eyes down to her feet and followed her mothers from the room.

She found them in the healer's quarters near the queens' residence.

"Lochlan, can you hear me?" Faolan's frantic voice rose above the din. "Do you have news of Alona?"

"Your Majesty, please give us room to help him," the healer insisted.

"How is he?" Brea peeked inside the crowded room.

"We don't know yet." Tierney joined her in the hall. "Hopefully he will wake soon and have news of Alona."

"Alona, of course," Brea murmured, but she was more worried about Lochlan. He was deathly pale, and she swore she could feel the heat coming off him from across the narrow room. She'd always seen him as invincible. Nothing could shake the obstinate man with the iron will. But now, he looked weak. Broken. Like a shell of himself. Brea worried he might not make it.

She turned away when the healer bared his open wound, casting the dirty bandages aside. Blood and infection oozed from his abdomen. Someone had run him through with a sword.

Brea was reminded of her own injuries and the infection that could have killed her if it wasn't for the man lying on the table now. He'd taken her to Loch Langt to cool her fever. She just prayed the healers had everything they needed to treat him half as well as he'd cared for her.

"Finn." The Queen consort ushered her out of the way to make room for Finn who was relying heavily on Emmet to get him into the room.

"What news do you have?" Faolan demanded, turning to the second injured man who was supposed to be as good as family to her. But the queen only had ears for Alona.

"She's in Gelsi." Finn collapsed on the bed in the corner of the room. "Queen Regan holds her in the dungeons."

"The dungeons? How dare she put a princess in the dungeons!" Tierney's face turned red to match her hair.

"How are you, Finn?" Brea asked over the queens' tittering about their lost daughter. "Are you injured? What do you need?"

"Water, food, and sleep. In that order. And maybe a bath." He groaned as he laid back on the cot.

Brea moved to sit beside him, pouring a cup of water for him. His lips were cracked and bleeding from too much time under Eldur's unforgiving sun. "Sip slowly." She cautioned him. "I'll find you some food soon."

"Where in the dungeons? Can we get to her?" Faolan demanded.

"I'm afraid not, your Majesty. Regan has her held deep

within the bowels of her palace. I'm told none can reach her from outside the palace."

"Well, we will have to find someone inside to help us." Faolan's shoulders stiffened with resolve. "That woman will rue the day she dared lay a hand on my daughter." Faolan swept out of the room, not bothering to ask the healers how Lochlan was doing.

"I think maybe I'll sleep now," Finn murmured. "Water, sleep, then food. I can bathe next week." He was fading quickly, but Brea knew she needed to get some more water in him first.

"Not so fast, Finny boy. Drink this." She refilled his cup and helped him sit up to drink it. "You can rest when this is empty."

"Where's Finn?" An older soldier barged into the room, his eyes zeroing in on Finn. "Tell me everything," he demanded.

"Listen, I don't know who you are, but he needs to rest. You can ask him your questions about the princess once he's had a chance to sleep. Come back in the morning." Brea glared at the man.

"I'm his father." The man moved to sit on the cot beside her. "Eamon Donovan, head of the Queen's guard."

"Oh." Brea focused on helping Finn sip from the cup. "I didn't realize."

"Don't apologize for championing my son, Lady Brea. He's lucky to have a friend like you. Can you tell me what happened? Where did you find him?"

"In the orchard." Brea recounted the details for Captain Donovan.

"And Loch?" He cast a worried glance at Lochlan's still form across the room.

"I don't know. They are still working on him."

"I'm glad you were there to help them." The captain took his son's hand.

"I'm okay, Father. Go see to the queens. They'll be worried about Lona."

"Get some rest. I'll come back tonight to check on you." The captain left, asking Brea to send word if anything changed.

Finn was asleep before Brea could set the empty cup on his bedside table.

Not knowing what else to do, Brea sat in a chair beside Finn's cot while the healers treated Lochlan's injuries. When they finally finished, Brea approached his bedside. "How is he?"

"The injury was severe, and the infection has spread beyond his wounds. The next few hours will tell us whether he will make it or not."

"You have magic. Isn't there anything more you can do?"

"We need to keep his temperature down. And keep him comfortable."

"Well, don't you have some kind of magical cooling blanket or something?"

"We do. It's called ice." The healer gave her a small smile.

"Is there anything I can do to help?"

"We have other patients to see to throughout the palace this evening. It will help if you can keep an eye on him. Keep the ice packs cold and change them the instant the ice melts."

"I can do that." Brea nodded. Taking the bowl of ice, she sat beside Lochlan's still form.

"I'm serious. You big fae brute, you better not die." Brea lifted a fresh cloth filled with ice from the bowl and draped it across his forehead. She didn't intend to move until he opened those midnight blue eyes and said something mean. Then she'd know he would be okay.

"Dear." Someone shook Brea's shoulder.

Her eyes slid open, and for a moment, she didn't remember where she was.

The healer. Finn. *Lochlan.* Rubbing her face, she looked to the man laying still on the bed wrapped in bandages and ice.

"Lady Brea," the voice said again.

She lifted her eyes to find Captain Donovan standing next to her chair. "You should go back to your rooms."

She shook her head, her eyes finding the empty bed where Finn had been resting. "Where's Finn?"

"I had a few men help him to his rooms where he'd be more comfortable. My son was unharmed, just exhausted. We do not yet know the extent of their journey, but it took a toll on him."

She nodded, settling her eyes back on Lochlan. "Will he wake?"

"The healer said his fever broke. We need to remove the ice."

"I can do it."

He shook his head. "You need sleep, my lady."

"No." She stretched her neck to the side. Sleeping in a tiny wooden chair wasn't fun. "I can't leave him alone." She didn't know why. Lochlan wasn't her friend. Most of the time, they couldn't stand each other. But he did this for Alona, was injured searching for her. Maybe Brea felt some sort of connection to the girl she'd been switched with, or maybe she just wanted to pay Lochlan back for saving her life when she was the one injured. She didn't like owing him anything. After this, they were even.

"Lady Brea." Captain Donovan sighed. "Your mothers would be vexed with me if I let you stay here all night."

She snapped her eyes to his. He knew? This man she'd never met before this day. "How?"

He seemed to understand her question. "I have been in this palace since I was a young man at the queen's side. There is very little that goes on I am not aware of."

"Does Finn know?" About her. About Alona.

He shrugged. "I do not know. Lochlan and I have been under strict orders to share our knowledge with no one, but my son is shrewd. Alona is like a daughter to me, my lady. I was with her when she was taken, and I have to live with that. But you I can protect, even if it's just from yourself.

The healer and her assistant will take care of Lochlan. I'm ordering you to go get some sleep."

She sighed and pushed to her feet. "Yeah, okay." Unable to take her eyes from Lochlan's distressed face, she released a breath. "Just..."

"I will have them inform you of any changes."

"Thanks." Turning, she made herself walk from the room and into the waking palace. Early morning sunlight streamed through archways, lighting the stone underneath her feet.

She was due at the stables soon, but she couldn't fathom being so far from Lochlan right now. Master Arturo would understand.

Sleep wasn't an option with the worry coursing through her, so she hurried to the courtyard she visited every morning to make a wish in the fountain. The wishes ranged from going back to the human realm to seeing Myles again to Lochlan returning.

This morning, there was only one.

She didn't have a coin on her, so she bent to pick up a pebble near the base of the fountain. Holding it in the palm of her hand, she closed her eyes.

Let Lochlan live.

Releasing the stone, she watched it hit the water with a satisfying plunk. This palace couldn't take another tragedy. For a month, they'd walked around in a fog of despair, trying to ignore the things they refused to talk about. Alona, gone. Finn, gone. Lochlan...

At least Finn was back with them in one piece.

But Lochlan... What would happen to her mothers if they lost another piece of themselves? The family in this palace had what Brea had always dreamed of. Two parents—three if one counted Captain Donovan—who truly cared about those under their watch. Alona grew up with Lochlan as the sibling Brea always wished she'd had.

And Finn, good, kind, Finn—the boy who could make anything better.

Alona may have been taken from her home as a baby just like Brea, but she got the better deal.

Brea trudged back to her room to find Rowena waiting for her with a too-bright smile.

"May I draw you a bath, Lady Brea?"

Brea grunted. "No."

"I'll fetch you something to eat then." She ran out the door before Brea could tell her not to come back.

Yanking off her boots, Brea took off yesterday's clothing and slipped on a comfortable sleeping gown before curling up on her bed. She slid the Humantales book toward her.

Reading stories that held some basis in human history brought tears to Brea's eyes. Would she ever see her world again? The cars and technology. People who didn't treat her as some fragile princess.

Netflix. Man, she missed Netflix.

And Amazon two-day shipping.

If she wanted to buy something she had no use for here, she'd have to make the effort of going to a shop. And everything was just so dang useful.

"Don't they know how to waste money?" she grumbled to herself.

It was probably the weariness speaking, but she hated this world of magic and kings and queens. Her magic sizzled underneath her skin, but she was too tired for it to become more than that.

She curled in on herself and hugged the book to her chest. Rowena returned with a silver tray laden with food.

"I brought you Eldur Brew." She winked, a satisfied grin on her face. "The queen's lady's maid told me you enjoyed it, so I snuck some up. We don't have to tell anyone of your lowborn tastes." She laughed as if it were some giant joke.

"I'm not hungry."

"Come now, Lady Brea. A good breakfast makes every morning brighter." She set the tray on the table next to the bed. "I'll even allow you to eat it in bed."

With a sigh, Brea rolled over and reached for the cup of Eldur Brew—coffee to her. "Is there any sugar?"

Rowen lifted a tiny silver spoon and scooped sugar into the Eldur Brew.

"More." Brea stopped herself. "Please."

Rowena nodded. "Today, I think you're going to need it."

"Lady Brea," Master Arturo snapped. "That is not your job."

She rolled her eyes and continued stabbing clumps of hay with a pitchfork. She'd planned to avoid the stables, but the longer she sat in her room with Rowena staring at her, the more restless she became.

"Chill. It's all good. We won't tell the queen."

He yanked open the stall door and crossed his arms. "A woman of your station does not muck stalls."

"Then what am I here for?" She threw the pitchfork, and it cracked against the wall. Her chest heaved. "Please, tell me why my m—the queen would allow me to work with you if there are so many freaking rules."

"My lady." Emmet jogged toward them. "Are you okay? I heard a crash."

"Wonderful. My babysitter is here." Brea was throwing a tantrum, but in her exhaustion, she didn't care. Working in the stables took her mind off the man who still hadn't woken, despite his fever breaking. It let her forget about this new crazy world she lived in where nobody left her alone.

She'd tried to sleep after breakfast, but her mind wouldn't quiet. Now, here she stood with no more than an hour of sleep in an uncomfortable chair, and Master Arturo and Emmet staring at her like she was back at the Clarkson Institute.

Magic sparked in her fingertips, but not enough to do more than tingle along her skin. Man, she needed rest.

She calmed her breathing. "I'm sorry." She ran a grimy hand over her sweaty hair. "I know I shouldn't be here doing this." Which seemed nuts to her after growing up on a farm and doing the dirty jobs her mom refused to do. She couldn't count the number of stalls she'd mucked with Myles.

Master Arturo bent to pick up the pitchfork she'd

thrown. "Lady Brea, the queen allowed you this apprenticeship against the judgement of others so you'd have something to occupy your time. But she was very clear. You are to learn about our breeding programs, the pride of Eldur. I can't have you going home to the palace each day with your clothing in dirty tatters and your face streaked with grime. It isn't proper."

She didn't care what was proper, but she realized it mattered to her. "I understand."

"Emmet, show her ladyship back to the palace. I think she's done for the day."

Emmet looked to her nervously.

With a sigh, Brea walked past him. "Let's go."

By the time they rode along the now familiar road, the sun had started to sink on the horizon. She wasn't sure where this day had gone, but she clicked her tongue, nudging the horse into a trot. The quicker she got back to the palace, the sooner she could check on Lochlan.

At the back gates near the kitchen, she dismounted and ran inside, weaving through the halls until she stood on the threshold of the healer's quarters. Glancing down at her dirty boots and pants, she cringed, knowing she probably smelled as bad as she looked.

Tucking an errant lock of hair behind her ear, she approached Lochlan's bed. His face was relaxed in sleep, but it had much more color than earlier in the morning. A breath rushed out of her. He was going to be okay.

"Lady Brea." Rowena stepped up beside her. "You just missed Finn. He was here speaking with Lochlan."

Brea's eyes widened. "Lochlan was awake?"

The maid nodded. "He's been in and out of consciousness all day. The healer claims that is quite normal."

"What are you doing here, Rowena?" She wasn't aware her maid knew Lochlan well.

Rowena shrugged, red creeping up her neck. "I've stayed most of the afternoon so I could give you a full report when you returned."

"Wait... you sat here for hours... for me?"

"Of course."

Brea stared at her maid with this new knowledge. She knew the woman had been with Alona for many years, but how had she so easily developed affection for Brea too?

"I think you like me, Rowena."

Rowena frowned. "Well, yes, you are my lady. I remember holding you in my arms on the day of your birth. No amount of grumbling or childish outbursts will erase that."

"Childish outbursts," Brea grumbled. No, she didn't grumble. Rowena wasn't right. Except, she sort of was.

"Come, Lady Brea." Rowena put a hand on her arm and guided her into the hall. "You need to bathe."

"Are you telling me I stink?"

"Yes."

A laugh burst out of Brea, a foreign sound after such a lousy day, but it felt good. She followed the strange maid without another protest.

Brea jerked awake, and cool water sloshed across the floor. She'd fallen asleep in her bath after telling Rowena to give her some peace. The woman tried to bathe her. Brea would never get used to all the nudity the fae thought nothing of.

The same thud that woke her sounded at the door again. Her brow creased. She stood, letting rivulets of water stream down her weary body. Every muscle ached as she stepped from the tub onto the cold stone floor, a puddle forming at her feet. She reached for the bath sheet and dried herself before shrugging on a silk robe. Twisting her hair in the towel, she approached the door and gripped the handle.

She wished Rowena was here to tell whoever it was to go away. How long had she been asleep? Moonlight filtered through the window, casting shadows across her bed.

Pulling the door open, she jumped back as a body rolled in. Someone had been slumped against the door. It only took her a moment to realize it was Lochlan staring up at her with hazy eyes.

"Loch." She shut the door and crouched down at his side. "What on earth are you doing here?"

"Had to..." He sucked in a breath. "Talk." His eyes slid shut. "What's wrong with... hair?"

"Huh?" Oh. She touched the towel on her head, suddenly self-conscious. "Come on, douchey Loch. Let's get you up."

He let her wrap his arm around her neck. "I needed to find you."

Her lips curved up as she heaved him to his feet. "Well, you did. In my room. In the middle of the night. Good job."

Stumbling under his weight, she crashed into the bed. He fell onto it, and she sighed. "Good a place as any." Noting his bare feet, she shook her head. Why would Lochlan escape from the healer and come to her rooms in the middle of the night? She highly doubted the healer let him go.

Straining, she pushed his legs onto the bed and checked his bandages to make sure they were still in place. "You shouldn't be here," she whispered.

His eyes slid open and fixed on her. "Brea." He tried to lift a hand, but it fell back to the bed. "It's Myles."

Her entire body froze. What could Myles possibly have to do with this place? With where Lochlan had been? She hovered over Lochlan, willing him not to say the words she feared more than anything.

But that was the thing about wishes. Whether they were made in a sparkling fountain with gleaming coins or in the darkness of the night with nothing but desperation, they rarely came true.

A wish was nothing more than a lie one told themselves.

Myles was okay.

He'd remain safe and alive.

She didn't need him.

All wishes. All lies.

Lochlan's voice cracked on his next words. "He's in Fargelsi. Queen Regan has him."

And all those wishes shattered, slicing through her heart like the fragile glass giving false protection to their hope.

Pain was part of this life. Lochlan experienced his fair share. He'd seen queens crumble and families torn apart. He'd felt the sharp tip of a blade pierce his flesh many times.

He'd lost Alona.

But the agony he saw, the pain he caused with his words, was unlike anything he could remember.

This human girl was strong, stronger than anyone else he knew. She'd been taken from her own world and thrown into a battle between queens, yet it was this news that finally broke her.

Her shoulders hunched forward almost as if she caved in on herself. Tears hung in her long lashes but didn't fall.

"How," she whispered, her breath shaking. "How did that woman get to Myles?" Anger sparked in her eyes, and she clenched her jaw. "Griff." She slid from the bed and paced the length of the room. She yanked the towel off her head and damp hair tumbled over her shoulders.

"Brea." He forced the word out past the pain in his chest. He still wasn't quite sure what happened or how he'd ended up back at the palace, only that Finn saved him.

But he did remember the weeks before their battle with the men from Iskalt.

Brea continued pacing and talking to herself. "He's dead. Griffin O'Shea doesn't deserve to be in the same world as Myles, let alone the same palace." She froze. "It's all my fault. He's here because of me."

"Brea." Lochlan tried and failed to raise his voice as a shiver wracked his body and he started convulsing. Pain shot through him, and the room faded away until all he could hear was "No, no, no."

Warm hands touched his bare chest above the bandage, and the feel of her grounded him, keeping him from sinking into the darkness.

"You're freezing cold." She yanked the blankets from under him and folded him in a warm cocoon. Still, he continued to shake. "Oh, for freak's sake."

Lochlan didn't know what she was doing until a warm body pressed up against his under the blankets. Her arms wound around him.

He wanted to protest, to push her away, but for the first time in hours, he started to warm.

"I saw this in a movie," she whispered, her breath hot on his shoulder.

Not even her wet hair bothered him as he let himself relax in the comfort. When was the last time someone hugged him? It was probably Alona, but that would have been ages ago.

He'd forgotten how nice it felt to have a caring touch.

But Brea didn't care about him, she couldn't. How could this girl learn to trust anyone in this world when the man she'd fallen for turned out to be nothing more than a manipulative liar?

They wanted the best for her. Lochlan, Finn, the queens. Everyone in Eldur would embrace Brea if she let them. But he could see it in her eyes every time she looked at him. She wouldn't believe anyone so easily again.

"Do you feel better?" she asked.

He couldn't speak.

"I kind of hope you forget this."

Of course she did. They weren't friends. He'd imagined her worry when he first returned injured.

"When I was in Fargelsi," she went on. "I refused to talk to Griff about Myles. It irritated him, but maybe some subconscious part of me knew. Myles is good, ya know?" Her voice quivered. "He doesn't deserve to be here. His family must be so worried. They love him. Unlike..."

She stopped talking, and he wanted more than anything for her to go on. He'd learned bits and pieces of how she grew up from checking in on her over the years at the queen's request. The humans who raised her didn't deserve such a strong, resilient daughter.

"Whenever things were bad at home, I'd climb out my

window and run across the fields separating our farm from Myles'. No matter what he was doing, he had this smile like he was always happy to see me, like I was never interrupting no matter what I needed. He was the only person who ever made me feel like I mattered."

Lochlan turned his head to rest his cheek on Brea's damp hair. She'd always mattered in the fae world, even after she was exchanged for Alona. The first time Queen Faolan sent him to check on her in the human realm, he was fifteen. He'd hidden behind a barn as he watched her lay in the grass gazing at the clouds with a boy by her side—probably Myles.

There'd been a simple kindness in her then, a kindness he hadn't seen since rescuing her from the swamp. But he saw it now in the way she lent him her warmth, in the way she spoke of her friend.

"It should be me," she whispered, the words barely audible. "Myles is trapped in Fargelsi, but it should be me."

Gathering his strength, Lochlan finally spoke. "It shouldn't be anyone. I need to tell you more." He sighed, knowing she wasn't going to like this. "I learned of Myles' fate from... Griff."

Her head shot up. "Explain."

Ignoring the pain speaking caused him, he went on. He owed her the words. "We spent weeks trying to find a way into Gelsi, but the magic on the border has been strengthened since your escape. Once, it only affected people of Fargelsian blood. Now, no one can cross without permission. One night, we were camped in the Vatlands and Griff came to us."

"Why would he do that?"

Lochlan sighed, remembering the letter Griff had given him for Brea. It sat at the bottom of his saddle bags that Finn had carried across his shoulder for the last part of his journey. "He said he cares for you, and you deserved to know. For what it's worth, he did look like he regretted his role in abducting Myles."

"It's worth nothing."

"I know." Giving her the letter would only cause her more pain. He'd have to wait until she had Myles back no matter how much it angered her.

She was quiet for a long moment, and pulses of warmth flooded him followed by searing heat. A cry left his lips, and he bucked up off the bed.

"What's wrong?" Brea sat up but didn't let go of him.

"How are you doing this?" His remaining strength evaporated, flowing from his mind to his body. The wound in his chest pulled together as the last of the infection oozed out, soaking the bandage. He yanked at the bandage. "Get it off me." It was suddenly too tight, and he couldn't breathe. The moon hung in the sky, it shouldn't have been possible for her Eldur magic to rise.

"I can't. You'll bleed."

"Brea," he growled.

"Fine." With deft hands, she unwound the bandage, her eyes going wide.

It took all his effort to lift his head and see that the wound was still there, though much smaller than it had been.

Brea sat back on her heels. "I don't understand."

"What were you feeling just then?"

"Sadness. Guilt. Some anger."

How was it possible she shrank his wound and pushed the infection from his body?

"I don't understand." Her voice was small.

He didn't either. Shrinking away from her, he pressed himself into the bed, wishing he had the strength to walk away. Brea Robinson had a power he'd never seen before, and he wasn't sure if the feelings rolling through him were excitement or fear.

Probably a little of both.

After the revelation, Lochlan fell into blissful darkness as his exhaustion won the battle. Brea didn't return to the bed, and he wondered if she was afraid of herself as well.

He woke gradually as one does when they have nowhere to be. Sunlight flickered across his skin, and he touched the wound to see if he'd been dreaming the night before. No, part of it had been healed.

It wasn't completely gone, and he wondered if that was only because Brea couldn't yet control the power. She turned eighteen soon and had to be taught.

As much as the girl frustrated him, he'd remember last night's kindness for a long time. He lifted his head, hoping to see her skittering about the room. A sleeping gown lay draped on the end of the bed, but other than that, there was no sign she'd ever been there.

That she'd ever laid beside him with her warm arms wrapped around him.

The door burst open and a familiar woman bustled in, a tray in her hands. "Lady Brea, I brought breakfast." Rowena circled the room before finally seeing him. Her jaw dropped open before her eyes narrowed. "Lochlan O'Shea, this entire palace has been searching for you all night."

He sighed and tried to sit up.

"No, no. You stay until we can get someone to help you. As it seems Lady Brea isn't here, you can eat her breakfast." She set the tray on the table next to the bed.

"I will not eat in bed." He finally managed to push himself up. "It isn't proper."

"Proper schmoper." She placed her hands on her hips.

He raised an eyebrow. "Is that one of Lady Brea's odd phrases?"

"Yes, and I quite enjoy it. If you get out of that bed, I'll go find the queen and tell her just where I found you this morning."

Lochlan met her gaze in a silent standoff before sighing. He'd never imagined eating in bed, but he could see he wasn't getting out of this.

Rowena handed him a cup of tea.

"Do you know where Brea would have gone before even receiving her breakfast?" he asked.

Rowena nodded. "Possibly. She could be in the stables."

"Why would she be in the stables?" A morning ride, perhaps?

"Her apprenticeship."

He coughed. The queen's daughter had an apprenticeship in the stables? Had this entire palace turned upside down while he'd been gone? "I must speak with her."

"Well, you can wait until she returns. You are in no shape to ride to the stables. I will find some guards to help you back to the healer—and we won't tell anyone where you've been." With one final eyebrow raise, she turned on her heel and left.

Lochlan groaned as he slumped out of bed. The healer would never believe what Brea's magic did to his wound.

Until he understood what it meant, no one could know.

He hadn't been able to protect Alona, but he refused to let anything happen to another Eldurian princess.

Not even when her name was Brea Robinson.

Because that girl was not going to make any of this easy.

"Go away." Brea rolled over on her bed and threw her blanket over her head. Everyone in the palace had knocked on her door over the last two days, but she refused to come out or let anyone in. She was so done with this place and everyone in it. After her one trip to the stables, she realized nothing could take her mind off Myles and decided she'd rather wallow in bed.

"Regan has Myles." She whispered the words that sounded impossible. Here she was on the other side of the fae world with no way to help him. No one could get inside Fargelsi now that Regan had completely sealed the borders.

"Lady Brea, get out of bed this instant." Rowena peeled the covers away from Brea.

"Ugh, how did you even get in here?" Brea had barred

the door on the inside and barricaded it with her dresser and half the furniture in her sitting room. It was all still piled in front of the door.

"I have my ways."

"You can walk through walls?" Brea's eyes widened.

"Walk through walls? You are in sore need of an education in magic." Rowena pulled her from the bed and steered her toward the bathroom. "Walk through walls, honestly."

"Then you can apparate?"

"Stop speaking nonsense words and get in the bath." Rowena already had the sunken tub filled with hot water and all manner of scented oils and flowers. "You will stop acting like a spoiled child and attend the ball this evening."

"Nope." Brea turned to retreat to her room. "I've had enough of fae parties to last me a lifetime. No thanks." She slammed the bedroom door behind her and slid the lock in place.

"You will attend this party as your mothers' guest."

Brea whirled around to find Rowena stripping her bed. "How are you *doing* this?"

"Get in the bath, Brea. You smell like one of your horses."

"Fine. But I'm not going anywhere, so you can go out however you came in." Brea stomped to the bathroom where Rowena had opened the doors and windows to let in the fresh air.

Stepping into the warm bath, Brea let out a moan as she sank up to her chin. The tub was large enough for four people and almost deep enough to be called a pool. Clearing her mind of all things Myles, she let herself relax in the bath, washing away days of sweat and tangles from her hair.

"That's enough, now. Time to get out." Rowena laid a bath sheet on the rack beside the tub and marched out of the room. "Hurry up child, we have to get you ready for the ball."

"I'm not going. Besides, isn't it still afternoon? Don't balls happen at night?"

"Not in Eldur. Here they happen at dusk. You have an hour to eat something and get dressed. The queens expect you in the courtyard at four."

"Whoever heard of a ball at four in the afternoon?" Brea slipped under the water to rinse her hair, contemplating not coming back up, if only to escape Rowena's ministrations. There was no way that woman wouldn't deliver Brea to the courtyard on time without a hair out of place if that was what Queen Faolan wanted.

"You will ride up to the gardens with the queens. Now, out with you."

Brea reluctantly left the safety of her bath and wrapped the bath sheet around her. She barely winced this time when Rowena used her magic to dry Brea's hair. Every drop of water from her hair splattered on the tile floor behind her, leaving her hair soft and dry.

"I need to learn that trick once my magic figures out what it's doing." She crossed her sitting room to the vanity that had only moments ago blocked the door. Rowena had moved everything back while she was in the tub.

"Sit."

"Yes ma'am." Brea flopped onto the chair, resigned to the fact that she was going to this ball tonight whether she wanted to or not.

"So what's this party about? We celebrating fae Flag Day now?" Brea had lived among the fae long enough to know they would use any excuse to throw themselves a party.

"I don't know what Flag Day is, but tonight we are celebrating your eighteenth birthday, and you are Queen Tierney's guest of honor."

"It's my birthday?" Brea slumped against her chair. She couldn't get out of this or ditch out early. Tierney had been nothing but nice to her. She owed it to her mothers to be there. "I've lost all track of time with the weird Fae calendar."

"Humans don't know how to keep the proper time." Rowena busied herself with Brea's hair. "I hear a rumor that they don't live long past one hundred."

"Most don't live that long."

"With all their fancy medicines and doctors, you'd think they'd be the ones to live the longest."

"How old are you, Rowena? If you don't mind me asking." She was a grandmotherly sort so Brea had always assumed she was in her seventies, but she was beginning to suspect Rowena might be the oldest person she'd ever met.

"One-hundred-and-eighteen on my last birthday."

"Wow. Will I live that long?" Brea picked at the scones on the tea tray Rowen brought for her. There was even a pot of Eldur Brew she poured for herself. She hadn't eaten anything in more than a day, and her stomach growled in angry protest.

"Oh you'll live much longer, I'm sure." Rowena tugged on her hair, twisting it into an elegant style she couldn't manage on her most patient day. "Royals always live longer than commoners."

"I'm not a royal." Brea sipped her coffee.

"You might not feel like one, love, but it doesn't change the fact that your mother is a queen, which makes you of her royal blood."

"I suppose all the nobles will be in attendance tonight?" Brea changed the subject anytime the conversation went anywhere near the word 'princess' in regards to herself.

"Birthday celebrations are a special occasion in Eldur. Tonight, commoners and nobles alike will dine with you and your mothers."

"Oh no," Brea groaned. All the commoners she'd met in the marketplace would know who she was by the end of the night. There would be no hiding her link to the palace now.

"That's right, the whole of Eldur will know you as Lady Brea after tonight." Rowena chuckled.

"And what must I wear?" Brea had visions of the ridiculous dresses she'd had to wear in Fargelsi and didn't relish the thought of donning a gown that weighed more than she did.

"It's a lovely sea foam green silk. I think you'll like it. The queen chose it for you. She said she wanted you to be comfortable."

Brea doubted that was possible, but she went through the

motions, putting on her underthings, surprised when Rowena skipped the corset.

Rowena held the dress aloft as Brea slipped it over her head. A cloud of soft sea foam silk fell around her, light as a feather. Long, sheer sleeves cascaded to the floor.

"There's a slit in the sleeves for your hands." Rowena helped her adjust the fitted sleeve that hugged her arms from the base of her shoulder to her elbows, leaving the rest to flutter behind her when she walked.

With a slit up to her hip, it was a far cry from anything Regan would have put her in.

"It's beautiful." Brea gazed at herself in the mirror. The simple dress left her shoulders bare, and it was as comfortable as her sleeping gowns. "Good job, Mom." She turned to admire the gold trim along the neckline and the gold sandals she would have worn in the human world.

Rowena had threaded a string of golden beads through her hair. It reminded Brea of a tiara, which she didn't like, but the effect was perfect for the dress.

"I guess I have a birthday ball to get to." Brea heaved a sigh. It was the last thing she wanted to do when her best friend probably sat in the dungeon in Fargelsi and didn't have a clue what was happening or why he was involved.

"Now, be on your best behavior and don't embarrass your mothers." Rowena held the door open for her.

"Thank you, Ro-Ro." Brea leaned down and kissed her rosy cheek.

"Oh, be on with you." Rowena shooed her down the hall to meet her mothers.

"Brea, darling you look lovely." Tierney crossed the courtyard to greet her. "Happy birthday, dear." She folded Brea into her arms, and she had to admit, Tierney gave the best hugs.

"We are so sorry to hear about your friend, Myles." Faolan linked her arm through Brea's. Both queens wore simple silk ballgowns adorned with exotic flowers in the queen's colors. Queen Regan wouldn't have deigned to wear something so simple, but both of Brea's moms looked lovely. "We will do everything we can to bring him and Alona back to us. I give you my word, he is every bit as important as Alona."

"Thank you ... Mom." Brea decided in that moment the name didn't feel awkward at all. "He is the most important person in my life. I can't sit back and do nothing to save him."

"We will figure this out, darling." Tierney linked her arm around Brea's free arm and together they headed to the carriage awaiting them. "But please, try to enjoy your party tonight. It was supposed to be a surprise, but we decided you probably wouldn't like that."

"Good plan." Brea laughed. It warmed something inside her that her mothers really were learning who she was and what she liked.

"Your eighteenth birthday is an important milestone, Brea," Faolan explained as their carriage rolled along the cobblestone streets. "In the next few days, your magic will begin to change, and you'll have more control over it. We've arranged for you to have a tutor to help you. You'll have lessons each afternoon once you return from your apprenticeship at the stables."

"Thank you both. I hadn't even realized it was my birthday. I've lost all sense of time since I arrived in the fae world."

"We hope you will one day think of Eldur as your home, but for tonight, we just want you to have fun and know that we are working to bring Myles home."

It was a relief to hear they realized how important he was. Not that Brea would ever stop worrying about him until she laid eyes on her best friend again.

"Lady Brea." Lochlan reached to help Brea down from the carriage.

"Loch, how are you feeling? Should you be here?"

"I wouldn't miss your birthday." His lips twitched. "With your lack of control, you're liable to set the whole place on fire. Wouldn't want to miss that."

"Very funny." She took his hand, noting how pale he was. Despite the facade of his fine clothing, he was in no shape to attend a ball. She'd only ever seen him in his black leathers or soldier's gear. Even in Fargelsi, he always wore simple black clothing.

But tonight, he was in full Eldur fashion, and Brea approved. His long fitted jacket matched the dark blue of his eyes. Trimmed in silver brocade with slitted sleeves, it fit him like a second skin. His sliver undershirt buttoned high, with a stiff collar, and his fitted trousers were of the same dark hue as his jacket. A pale blue and silver sash tied at his waist, accentuating his broad shoulders and narrow hips.

Following the queens, Brea walked silently beside him through the tiered garden, up to the highest level, her arm tucked tightly around Lochlan's. They passed commoners and merchants, each bowing as the queens strolled past. Cool breezes swept through the crowds as if called here by magic, which was probably the case. Fires in a rainbow of colors danced in the braziers as the sun met the horizon.

"Isn't it odd to have a ball so early in the evening?"

"Not in Eldur," Lochlan said with a frown. "Surely someone has taught you that much about Eldurian magic?"

"I still know nothing." Brea shrugged.

"I thought Griff taught you how Eldurians draw their magic from the sun."

"And in Iskalt, you draw your magic from the moon. And in Fargelsi, from nature." Brea remembered that much, though she didn't know what it meant.

"So, if your people harness magic from the sun, and mine from the moon, what would be the logical conclusion?" Lochlan pushed her to find the answer for herself.

"Oh!" She gazed around the gardens at all the obvious displays of magic, and it clicked. "They can only use their magic during the day?"

"And I can only use mine at night. But, at dawn and again at dusk, we are both powerful."

"What does that mean for Fargelsi?"

"They can use their magic anytime, which grants them a certain advantage, but they are not nearly as powerful as Iskalt and Eldur."

"I see."

"Now that you are of age, it is important that you learn to harness your magic."

"The queens have arranged for a tutor." Brea and Lochlan followed the queens to their thrones for the evening. They took up their place behind the queens on the dais. It was all so familiar. Brea fought the urge to yawn, pasting on her fake smile instead.

Nobles and commoners alike came to wish the Lady Brea a happy birthday, offering her little trinkets and baubles from the finest gold to the most common beads and stones. Brea found she preferred the simple gifts from the common folk. They were more heartfelt. A young woman shyly offered her a fuzzy white baby pigmy goat Brea refused to let out of her sight.

"You're supposed to eat that, you know." Lochlan stared at the baby goat in her lap. "It's delicious roasted with rosemary and onion."

"Shut your face, Lochlan O'Shea." Brea held her hands over the baby goat's ears. "Her name is Rosie, and she's my pet." Brea scratched the goat's head eliciting a lazy bleat.

"If you're going to keep that thing in your rooms, you need to get it a friend. There's nothing more destructive than a bored goat."

Brea leaned forward to ask her mothers if she could explore the gardens.

"Don't go far, dear," Tierney said. "We have an announcement to make soon, but take Lochlan with you."

Brea left the dais with Rosie in her arms, not overly concerned if Lochlan followed her or not. She made her way through the crowd, offering smiles and nods to those who looked like they wanted to talk, but she kept moving until she saw a familiar face near the buffet.

"Breee-anne of Tarth," Finn slurred, sipping from a flask. "How's the birthday girl?"

"I'm fine, thanks, but you're clearly drunk." She took his flask away, taking a sip of the contents for herself. "Yuck, that tastes like burnt leaves. Try the champagne.

It's delicious." Brea snagged two glasses from a passing waiter.

"Don't mind if I do." Finn poured a healthy splash of his flask into the champagne flute.

"Leave him be, Brea." Lochlan took her glass of champagne from her and drained its contents in one gulp.

"Hey, that was mine."

"I've seen what happens to you after you've had too much fae wine. I don't relish taking another swim in the fountains tonight."

"It happened one time." Brea turned toward Finn, ignoring Lochlan.

"What's wrong, Finn?"

"What's right?" He laughed, his eyes red rimmed like he hadn't slept much since his return.

"It's Alona's eighteenth birthday too, Brea," Lochlan said sadly.

"Oh, right. I'm sorry, Finn. I know you miss her. We'll get her back. Myles too, if I have anything to say about it."

"How?" Finn turned frantic eyes on Brea. "How can we get them back when they're fully out of our reach?"

"Brea, leave him alone," Lochlan moved to stand between them. "You don't know what he's lost. What any of us have. You can't possibly understand."

"I can't?" She gave him a shove. "I don't know what it's like to lose the most important person in my life? I can't understand how utterly helpless everyone feels about poor Princess Alona? Screw you, Lochlan O'Shea."

Brea stormed away, making her way back to the dais to sit with her mothers. Alona's mothers. She might have been born of Faolan's body, and they might be trying to force a family bond with her, but at the end of the day, Alona was the one everyone wanted, not her.

"May I have your attention, please?" Queen Faolan tapped her champagne flute. "Tonight is a special night. Princess Alona's eighteenth birthday. Though she isn't with us, our hearts and minds are always with her in her captivity."

"Why did I ever think this party was supposed to be about me?" Brea turned to leave. She didn't need to be here for this.

"But tonight is even more special because we have a very important guest of honor here with us."

Brea stopped long enough to catch her mother's eyes, pleading with her to stay.

"Some of you know her as Lady Brea Robinson, guest of the queens. But may I present her as Princess Brea Robinson—"

"How could she?" Brea wanted to disappear. She wasn't ready for this. She wasn't some kind of replacement for princess Alona.

"—Of Fargelsi."

Wait, what? Brea turned accusing eyes on her mother.

"Brea is the rightful heir to the Fargelsi throne. Yet the false queen has kept her prisoner there for years. Brea has recently escaped the clutches of our greatest enemy and has come to Eldur to help us fight. With Brea's help, we will bring Princess Alona home, and we will work together with our allies to bring an end to Regan's reign of terror and place the rightful heir—and ally—on the throne." Faolan lifted her glass to the cheers from the crowd.

There it was. The third shoe dropping right on her head just when she wasn't expecting it. With Faolan as her Eldurian mother and Lord Brandon as her Fargelsian father, she would always be a pawn to these people.

Noblemen and courtiers crushed around Brea, vying for her attention even more now than they had before.

"Please, excuse me." Brea hung her head. Clutching Rosie in her arms, she let the crowd sweep her away from the queen. Her mother. The woman who just betrayed her and settled one more lie on the house of cards that was Brea's life.

That house of cards crumbled around her like a pile of ashes.

Brea didn't stop until the brick path beneath her feet turned to grass. Looking up, the last rays of the sun began to fade away, and the party was in full swing behind her. Stumbling across the grassy lawn surrounding the tiered garden, Brea made her way toward the familiar building in the distance. The stables were her favorite place in the whole city. Her one refuge that made her feel normal.

"Lady Brea?" Master Arturo frowned at her dress, the tears in her eyes and the goat in her arms. "You know what? I don't want to know. Come with me."

"Sir?" Brea stumbled after him, her heels sinking into the soft dirt.

"You said you wanted to know when Raven was ready to give birth."

"Really? She's having the twins now?"

"Yes, and I could use your help. Just don't tell the queen I had you do anything beneath your station. And don't get that pretty dress dirty. You can find an apron and boots in the storage closet."

"Where can I put my goat?"

"'In the stewpot' is probably not the answer you're looking for, is it?" The stable master rolled up the sleeves of his fine tunic, and she realized he probably came from the party too.

"No." Brea put a protective hand over Rosie's head.

"Put her in the last stall with Penny. She'll take care of

her." Penny was Arturo's faithful dog who liked to mother all the creatures she came upon.

"Thank you, Master Arturo. I'll be quick." Brea darted for the supply closet, eager to visit Raven and meet her twin foals who would likely share Brea's birthday with her and the great princess Alona.

Raven paced the length of her stall, her long tail swishing back and forth. Brea stood frozen on the other side of the stall door. How did she get here? She'd ridden horses most of her life. But birthing one? Memories assaulted her of her last day with Myles. They sat in class talking about his horse, Captain, a mare who'd given birth while Brea was at the Clarkson Institute. But Myles wouldn't have stood back, frozen in fear.

No, he'd be in there comforting her.

Master Arturo busied himself laying fresh straw. "The straw has to be clean," he explained. "So it won't stick to the foals."

Brea nodded as if she took in every one of his words, but white noise invaded her mind. Myles should be there, not her. He'd have loved working in the stables and birthing horses.

Master Arturo continued talking. "We shouldn't have to do much to help her. Horses are amazing creatures and can do this pretty much on their own."

"What's happening?" a deep voice said over Brea's shoulder, a voice she'd recognize anywhere.

"What are you doing here, Loch?" He wasn't exactly the kind to hang out in barns or care whether a horse gave birth safely. In fact, she didn't know if he cared about anything at all. Well, except Alona.

"You left the party, and I..." He rubbed the back of his neck.

"You what?" She didn't have the energy for his vague words, not with the twins coming and the worry about Myles consuming everything she was.

"I don't know."

"Brea," Master Arturo called. "I need you to come tie Raven's tail."

Brea threw a look over her shoulder at Lochlan. "Maybe you should figure it out. Excuse me, I have something much more important to do than sit at another party." As if the words lent her strength, she pushed open the stall door and entered the wide space. Since getting pregnant, Raven had been kept in the front stall which was three times as large as the others.

Considering the pacing pony for a moment, Brea pulled a ribbon from her own hair and approached. "Hey, girl." She offered her a kind smile and reached out to run a hand down her velvety neck. "You're going to be just fine."

Raven stopped moving, letting Brea draw her hand down her back. "Myles used to tell me horses were much more intelligent than us. More kind. More courageous. I think he was right." She released a shaky breath as she thought of her friend. If she could believe her moms at all about Myles being just as important to rescue as Alona, she'd see him again.

The problem was she didn't know how much she trusted them. Alona was just an idea to her, some girl who got to live the life that should have been Brea's. She didn't know her. But Myles... he was a part of her.

Using the ribbon, she tied up Raven's tail, and she could imagine why Master Arturo insisted on it.

"Okay, Brea," he said. "Now, we must back away and give her space so we don't add to her stress. I am going to fetch a couple of stable boys from the party. You stay here and watch. We fae have many kinds of magic, but this here is unlike any other you'll see."

He hurried from the stall and down the long hall. Brea kept the stall door open as she stood on the threshold.

"Where is your goat?" The sound of Lochlan's voice made her jump. She hadn't realized he was still there.

"The dog is goat sitting."

"Because that doesn't sound ridiculous at all."

Brea jerked her gaze toward Raven as the pony lay down and rolled onto her side. Brea looked toward the barn door, hoping to see Master Arturo appear, but no one came.

"It's happening," she hissed. Where was Myles when she needed him?

"It can't be happening," Lochlan whispered back. "We're the only ones here."

"I don't think Raven cares about that."

The pony let out a groan.

"I think she's pushing. What do we do?" Brea bounced on her toes as magic tingled in her fingertips, latching onto her fear and excitement.

"Calm down." Lochlan gripped her arm. "Even I can feel your magic building. You don't want to scare Raven."

He was right. Brea clenched her fists at her sides, surprised when the power obeyed her and shrank away. They hadn't been lying to her. It was her eighteenth birthday, and she truly did have more control.

They continued to watch Raven until Master Arturo's voice called to them. "I'm here! I'm here!"

Brea glanced behind him but saw no stable boys. "Where's your help?"

He huffed as he reached them. "Not in any state to help with a birthing." His scowl told them everything they needed to know.

The stable boys he could find were drunk.

"It seems you two will have to assist."

Lochlan's eyes widened. "I don't—"

"Of course, we will." Brea shot Lochlan a look. He may be a prince of Iskalt and the Eldur queen's surrogate son, but that wouldn't save him tonight. "Tell us what you need us to do."

"Well, first, we wait."

Lochlan stood tense beside Brea as they watched Raven strain until two feet appeared.

"What do we do?" Brea whispered.

"Patience, my lady." A gleam shone in Master Arturo's eye.

When Brea was told she could spend her time in the stables instead of bored at the palace, she'd never imagined she'd get to witness something like this. As more of the foal's legs appeared, she leaned forward, not wanting to miss a single thing.

Master Arturo was right. This was a truer kind of magic.

Sliding the stall door open, Master Arturo entered slowly. "Push, girl." He looked back over his shoulder as if considering Brea. "All right, my lady. You can come in."

Brea almost wished he hadn't let her. What if she messed this up like she had a tendency to mess everything else up? The lantern flickered, casting shadows on the walls as she moved. If she knew how, she'd have used magic to light up the entire stall. But her magic was useless in the face of such an enormous task. Bringing a life—two lives—into the world.

"Brea, you need a cloth to grip the foal's legs."

She looked back at Lochlan and pursed her lips. "Give me your jacket."

For once, he didn't argue with her. He slid the dark jacket down his arms and held it out to her.

Master Arturo shook his head. "We have horse blankets you can use."

She smirked and dropped her voice so only he could hear. "I know."

With a shake of his head, he crouched down and gestured for her to follow suit, speaking softly the entire time. "Okay, Lady Brea, grip the foal's legs but don't pull. You need to wait for her to push, and then you apply pressure."

A slimy sack covered the legs, and Brea held back bile rising in her throat. She could do this. For Raven. But also for Myles. He'd be proud of her.

They went through cycles of Raven pushing and Brea helping the foal out before Master Arturo finally told her it was okay to pull. Once the shoulder was out, the rest came more easily until there was a new black pony in Eldur.

"It's a girl." Master Arturo grinned. "Lochlan, we need your help. There's still one more."

Lochlan reluctantly entered the stall. "W-what do I need to do?"

"Fetch a blanket from the stack I put at the other end of the stall and rub the foal down. Make sure she's completely free of the sac."

Brea didn't get the satisfaction of watching Lochlan actually do work in the stables because Raven started pushing again.

Before long, two new female ponies lay on their sides in the clean straw, one white and one black.

Brea rubbed the white one down, cleaning her black socks. She glanced up, meeting Lochlan's eyes as the black pony rested her head in his lap.

The smock Brea wore didn't protect her gown from getting filthy, but she no longer cared. It didn't matter that the woman calling herself her mom just revealed to all of Eldur that Brea was an escaped Fargelsian princess, or that she knew without a doubt they wished Alona had been sitting in her place.

Even her fear for Myles faded away for this moment, a moment she shared with Lochlan O'Shea of all people. Her cheeks burned as she remembered helping him heal, and the feel of his skin against hers.

She shifted her eyes away, not wanting to see him as more than the entitled prince she thought he was. Arrogant. Cruel.

Also protective.

The white pony—it would need a name—climbed to its feet, its legs wobbling slightly. She looked at Brea, her wide amber eyes seeing past the false smiles and sarcasm, almost like she could read the fear in Brea's heart. She nudged the side of her head, and that was it.

Brea Robinson was in love.

Brea didn't know how long she stayed at the stables, but she trudged back toward the palace with Lochlan at her side, wishing they'd decided to ride. Exhaustion from the day's events tugged at her, both good and bad.

She couldn't face anyone at the palace—not with the way

she ran from her own party—least of all her moms. She was grateful Lochlan didn't insist on speaking. He was a silent presence beside her, and for once, she didn't want to argue with him. Watching him care for the foal would be the image of him she'd hold onto each time they went to battle against each other, each time he annoyed her to the point of rage.

Rowena met them at the gates, her arms crossed over her chest. "Where have you been, my lady?"

Brea sighed. "Have you been waiting for me here all night?"

"Of course not. A guard saw the two of you coming up the path. Your mothers were quite distressed."

"Rowena," Lochlan barked. "Not tonight. Lady Brea was assisting me with an important matter. You can tell that to the queen."

Brea looked to him in shock. He was... helping her?

Rowena, looking thoroughly chastised, backed down. "Yes, of course, sir."

Lochlan trudged past them, his soiled jacket draped over one arm like a badge of honor.

"I need a bath, Rowena." Brea glanced down at her ruined gown. "And a way to destroy this without my moms taking notice."

To her maid's credit, she didn't worry over the dress. "So, where were you two, really?" She lifted a brow.

"Birthing two ponies."

Rowena stopped walking. "I was... not expecting that."

"What were you expecting?" Brea asked.

"Something sordid." Brea's face must have shown her disgust because Rowena laughed. "I found him in your bed, Brea. It's not that odd for me to think there is something betwixt you."

"Betwixt us?" Brea covered a laugh with a cough and nodded to the guards at the door before passing them. "I'm not even sure Loch has feelings, and certainly none for me."

"Your moms once held hope for him and Alona."

Brea raised a brow. "Okay."

"Without magic, Alona was—is—destined to join the serving class. She cannot take over her mother's rule as queen. But, she could marry a king and be saved her fate."

"And Loch is the rightful heir to the Iskalt throne." It made sense. "So, why did they give up that hope?"

"He changed. The queen began sending him on missions no one other than her knew the meaning of when he was fifteen. He'd be gone for weeks at a time and never came back the same. After that, he wouldn't entertain the thought of courting Alona."

They reached Brea's room, and Rowena got to work starting a bath, but Brea wanted to know more. Lochlan, the man who'd lost his parents and his throne when he was four years old only to be given to a foreign kingdom. The one who called his own brother an enemy but would do anything to save Alona.

And, of course, the man who'd held a newborn pony and looked more content than she'd ever seen him.

That guy was a contradiction, and unraveling his secrets

would be the perfect distraction to keep from thinking of Myles every moment of every day.

"Lochlan O'Shea," she whispered. "Who are you really?"

Brea could've stayed with the new ponies all day, but Master Arturo insisted she go back to the palace for lunch. She'd been there since dawn, not wanting to leave.

The stable boys—or men, she supposed since they weren't very young—worked under the harsh eye of their Master. He hadn't forgiven them for their antics three days ago.

She felt kind of sorry for them, but also thankful because their absence meant she got the coolest experience of her life.

She rode one of the horses back to the palace with Emmett trailing behind and passed the reins off to him after dismounting in the courtyard.

Her stomach rumbled, but she refused to go to the great hall for lunch. Her moms would be there, and she hadn't spoken to them since they revealed her Fargelsian heritage without her knowledge. That wasn't their secret to tell, but what did they care? She might be related to her mom by blood, but she wasn't her daughter, not truly. You couldn't force a family connection no matter how hard you tried.

She could have Rowena fetch her lunch, but found herself standing outside the library instead of her own rooms. It was her favorite place in the palace other than her wishing fountain. When she stood among the tall shelves of books, she could pretend she was back in the world she'd grown up in.

When she flipped through human books she'd never considered reading before, she could almost believe nothing had changed and that her best friend was preparing to talk her ear off about the newest story he'd soared through.

Maybe that was the real reason she loved it here. It reminded her of Myles.

She skimmed a finger along familiar spines as she wound through the stacks to reach the nook at the back, only to find she wasn't alone.

Finn lounged on the pillow-covered bench with Harry Potter and the Order of the Phoenix open on his lap. It was such an odd sight in this land, she couldn't contain the laugh that bubbled up.

Finn jerked his head up. "Oh, it's you."

She hadn't seen him since he was drunk at her party, and she suspected he was avoiding the world just like her. "Don't you work?" She hopped up onto the end of the bench. "You're part of the queen's guard, right? The troops your father leads?"

He nodded and snapped his book shut. "They do give us time off occasionally."

"Oh." She pursed her lips, unsure what more to say to him. A strange sense of déjà vu struck her, and she realized it was because they're been in this predicament once before, both seeking solitude in the library and finding each other instead. Maybe it meant they were... friends. She so desperately needed a friend right now. She'd cling to just about any thread of kindness.

A sigh rattled from his lips. "Brea... I haven't gotten the chance to tell you how sorry I am about your friend."

She looked away. "Yeah... thanks." Her eyes glassed over, but she blinked away the tears. "I'm sorry Alona wasn't here for her birthday." *Their* birthday.

He stared down at the book in his lap. "This was her favorite."

Brea scooted closer. "Why?"

"She thought it was hilarious humans thought magic worked this way."

Brea laughed. "But we—I mean they—don't. It's just a story, fiction. Humans don't believe magic exists at all."

"Like the muggles."

She bit back a grin. "Yes, like the muggles."

"When Lochlan brought human books back from their world, it was almost like he wanted to see how humans thought. I always wondered if the gifts meant more, if he..."

"Loved Alona?"

Finn nodded. "Even when Loch and I were sort of together—"

"Wait." She put a hand up. "Hold on. You cannot just drop this bomb and keep talking."

"Bomb?"

So many questions rolled through her mind. "So, you and Loch, like... dated?"

"I don't know what dating is, but we were young boys. You forget, Brea, that fae are—"

"Pansexual dreamboats? Yeah, I've been told. I'm just trying to picture it. Lochlan is so... Lochlan. And you're basically perfect."

He shook his head. "Lochlan is more than you think he is. When we were trying to find a way into Fargelsi, we were attacked."

"And you saved him by getting him back to Eldur."

He nodded. "After he took a sword for me."

She didn't know what to say to that.

"Lochlan and I never had real feelings for each other, but he is one of the few people I want beside me as long as I live."

"And Alona is the other." By the way people talk in this palace, she was a saint everyone loved. Brea tried not to resent her.

Finn rubbed a hand over his face. "Have you ever felt like your soul had been ripped from your chest? It's a hopelessness, a knowledge that you can't do a thing to save the most important fae in your life." A tear trickled down his cheek, and Brea remembered a similar question he'd asked her the first time they sat here.

Have you ever loved someone so much it killed you when they were gone?

You feel as if you're no longer alive, like your heart refuses to beat until you see them again.

We wish the pain away in the same breath we hold on to it as a reminder of what they were to us.

And yet, nothing had changed since then. Finn and Lochlan's mission to the border only ended in more pain.

Brea scooted closer and wrapped an arm around his shaking shoulders. "I know exactly what that feels like, Finn," she whispered.

He lifted his eyes to hers, and she saw herself staring back. Her fear. Her guilt.

"This Myles," he started. "You love him as much as I love her, don't you?"

She nodded. "Not romantically, but it's just as strong. Finn, he's my only family."

He leaned his head against hers. "Not your only family."

"If you mean the moms I don't know, don't say it. They just want Alona back. This isn't my home, Finn."

He held out his hand palm up. "Take my hand."

She threaded her fingers through his.

He squeezed her hand. "We can be each other's family. You and I... we'll get them back, Brea."

"We have to. I thought I killed Myles once, and it was unbearable. But now, I will do anything to save him."

"When the time comes, Brea, I'll help you. That's my promise. No matter what, I'll make sure you get him back."

She sniffled. "And I'll do whatever I have to do to bring Alona home to you."

Finn wasn't the first person in this world to make a promise to her.

But he was the first person she knew in her heart wouldn't break it.

Rowena eventually found Brea in the library and brought lunch to her and Finn. They stayed there flipping through books and sharing stories of Alona and Myles. It was better than any kind of therapy.

For the first time, she felt like someone truly had her back.

Not her aunt or her moms. Not the boy she'd started falling for in Gelsi or the one who drove her insane in Eldur.

Finn was nothing more than a soldier, a friend.

He was what she needed.

"When Alona comes back," she started. "I want to convince the queen she should get one of the new ponies as a welcome home present."

Finn smiled. "She loved being around the horses."

"Loves. We aren't allowed to talk in past tense. I've told you this before." It was the first inkling that Brea and Alona had anything in common. "I hope she likes me."

"She will. Alona is kind. She can make you feel like the most important fae in Eldur."

The door to the library opened, and footsteps sounded

on the other side of the stacks before Lochlan came into view, a scowl on his face.

"I looked for you two at lunch."

Brea shrugged and gestured to the tray of half-eaten food on the table. "We're not exactly in the mood for palace goings on."

Lochlan looked from Finn to Brea, his frown deepening. "Both of you have been avoiding me as well as the queens."

"Not in the mood for a lecture." Finn stood, leaving his book behind. "Brea, I won't forget that promise." He walked off, leaving Brea and Lochlan staring at each other while his steps faded away.

"What promise?" Lochlan asked after another beat of silence.

Brea got to her feet. "It's not important." For some reason, she wanted to keep the deal she'd made with Finn secret. Lochlan would probably call such a promise reckless, but he didn't know how empty either of them felt. Brea understood Finn on a level she'd never expected. "Why were you looking for me? Want news on our girls?"

"They're not our girls," he scoffed. "Those ponies belong to the kingdom until they're sold."

"I will not allow them to be sold." Her jaw clenched. "If you can just forget how it felt holding them in your lap when they came into the world, you're colder than I thought."

"I never claimed to be anything other than cold. I'm not your friend, Brea."

"Noted." She looked away, trying not to think of him

coming to her room injured or seeking her out in the barn. When she met his gaze again, a storm brewed in his eyes.

"Your mother has asked me to help with your magic."

"You're my tutor?" She brushed by him. "Hard pass."

"You don't have a choice in this."

She twisted on her heel, coming face to face with him. "Right, I forgot. I don't have choice in anything."

His gaze hardened. "You are eighteen now, of an age to control your powers. Powers we know nothing about. You did a partial healing on me, something I haven't ever seen. Your blood is half Fargelsian and half Eldurian. The rarest of mixtures when Gelsi does not allow its citizens to cross borders." He leaned down so their faces were closer. "We. Do. Not. Know. What. You. Can. Do." He bit out each word. "Do you understand how dangerous that is?"

She shrank away from him and his blazing eyes. "It's daytime. Can't you only use magic at night?"

"I do not need to use magic to test yours or to teach you further control. You do not control magic, Brea. That is impossible. But magic is fed by emotions, amplifying them. And those, our *feelings,* can be controlled."

Her entire life, she'd felt the power whenever she was angry or scared or sad. Her shoulders slumped as she realized Lochlan was right. She didn't want to feel like this any longer.

She couldn't.

Because it wasn't going away.

Brea was fae, and she had magic. Two truths she could no longer ignore.

Heaving a sigh, she met Lochlan's gaze once more. "I need help." She couldn't admit he was right, but this was as far as she went.

He nodded, his expression softening. "We start now." He moved to walk away but stopped and turned back to her. "We will understand your power, Brea. I won't let it overwhelm you." He opened his mouth to say more but shut it and nodded before walking to the door.

"Thank you," she whispered, too quiet for him to hear.

"Where are we going?" Brea jogged to catch up with Lochlan's long stride.

"The orchard. No one will bother us there."

"Ohh, let's go visit the ponies." Brea skipped ahead of him along the dirt path.

"Focus, Brea. This is important. You can go visit your ponies after training.

"You're no fun, Douchey Loch."

"I feel that word is more of an insult than you've led me to believe."

"I promise, among humans it is a great compliment. You might not be much fun, but I greatly appreciate your dedication to my training, oh great douchey one." She could barely keep a straight face, but the way his shoulders drew back and his big head swelled even more, he bought it. He made it too easy sometimes.

"It is my pleasure to help you, Brea."

She really wasn't looking forward to this. Her magic scared her. It was too unpredictable, and Lochlan was about to push her into using her magic on purpose.

Lochlan ignored her, coming to stop among the massive fire-nut trees. She'd recently learned the Brazil-nut-like trees had started to smolder and burn as the fire-nut pods began to ripen. In the coming weeks, the pods would burn away, leaving just the seeds behind.

"It's cooler in the courtyard." Brea fanned her face with her hands. The sun was just beginning to meet the horizon, but it was still hotter than Death Valley up there without the breezes that rushed through the canyon.

"Do you really want an audience to see you try to hone your magic?" Lochlan smirked at her.

"No, not particularly." She leaned against a tree trunk and yelped, jumping away from the hot surface.

"There's a reason they call them fire-trees."

"Noted." Brea brushed at her back to make sure she hadn't singed her clothes. "So how does this work when I have zero control over my magic?"

"That is lesson number one." Lochlan stood across the clearing from her. "You don't control the magic. Forget everything you think you know about magic. It's all human nonsense."

"Okay, so how do I make it do what I want?"

"Your magic is linked to your emotions. You will learn to

guide your magic by controlling your emotions, which is not going to be easy for you."

"Why me specifically?" He was already irritating her with his know-it-all attitude, like she should just know this stuff when no one had ever bothered to teach her.

"Humans let their emotions rule them. It's their biggest fault and our biggest challenge to break you of their bad habits."

"Well, I'm sorry." Brea crossed her arms over her chest. "We can't all be emotionless robots like the great *douchey* Lochlan O'Shea." Magic sizzled at her fingertips, itching to get out.

"Control your anger, Brea." Lochlan circled her. "Feel it. Experience the emotion. But don't let it rule your actions."

"And exactly *how* am I supposed to do that?" She could feel the difference in her magic now. Before, it was always a flash of awareness, a tingle just beneath her skin. This was more. This was big.

"Take a deep breath." Lochlan stood in front of her. "Close your eyes and focus." He moved in even closer to whisper in her ear. "And admit you find me handsome."

"What?" Brea's eyes snapped open, and the magic blazed hot within her, like a fire. For the first time, she realized that was probably why they called Eldur the fire realm. It wasn't about the hot temperatures, desert terrain, or even the fire plains and the dormant volcano. It was the fire that burned within its people.

"Admit it." Lochlan moved to sit on the ground, lounging back like they were at a picnic.

"You're infuriating. I'll admit that." Brea's head throbbed with the heat of her magic.

"Focus, Brea. Control the emotion. Your magic is linked with your anger. It's different for everyone. Different emotions drive our magic. Some more than others. I'm not sure anger is the right emotion, but your magic responds to it quickly ... and it's more fun for me." He propped up on his elbow.

"You're a jerk." A burst of energy left her body, slamming into the tree trunk behind Lochlan. An avalanche of smoking fire-pods rained down on his head, bouncing like coconuts off his skull.

Lochlan cursed, slapping a hand over his head where his blond hair singed.

"You're right, this is fun." Brea sat down pretzel style in the thick green grass, dragging one of the pods closer to her. "Thanks for the snack." She cracked open the pod and shook out the warm toasted nuts.

"They aren't ripe yet." Lochlan massaged his head.

"Tastes good to me." Brea popped another nut in her mouth.

"Yeah, they do, but they'll give you rancid bad breath for days when they aren't ripe."

"Of course." Brea dropped the pod, already tired of this game.

"When you've felt your magic before, what other emotion really seems to respond? And be honest. Remember, I am trying to help you."

Brea knew the answer, but she didn't want to tell him.

"I don't know, anger seems to work pretty well." Brea got to her feet. "Why don't we try that one again since you're so good at pissing me off."

"But you aren't capable of reeling that emotion back in. We should try something else." Lochlan rose to stand in front of her. "We need to find something easier to work with now, and then we can work up to anger. That's always the hardest emotion to control."

"Fine." Brea took a step back. "Fear. It always gets me."

"We can work with fear." Lochlan nodded, pacing back across the clearing. "Is it fear in general or more like fear for your life?"

"Fear in general usually has the magic buzzing under my skin pretty quickly. It's a little different than anger. It's intense, but not as ... sharp. Anger is more of a quick flash."

"Fear holds more promise," Lochlan said. "What do you fear the most?"

"Do you really have to ask?" Brea shot him a glare.

"Myles. Right."

"And don't you dare think of using him as some sort of training tool."

"You really do think the worst of me, don't you?"

"The fire-nut doesn't fall far from the tree."

"I am not my brother. Or my uncle. And neither of them are half the man my father was." Lochlan took a step toward her. "I wouldn't dare use your best friend just to push your magic to the surface. I know what he means to you."

"You couldn't possibly know."

"Right, I don't know what it's like to lose the most important fae in my life." He gave her words from the previous night right back to her. "Alona is my Myles, Brea. Trust me, I know."

"And we're back at anger." The sharp edge of her magic prickled under her skin, and she tried to control the emotion, but it was like trying to catch smoke.

"Look at me, Brea." His voice sounded in her ear, and she looked up into his dark blue eyes. His arm slid around her waist, and he pulled her close. "We're working on fear," he reminded her as his mouth claimed hers. The warm kiss was brief, but it did the job. Fear pulsed in her veins, and her magic bubbled up to the surface like a pot boiling over.

Brea gasped as she stepped back and her palm—flashing with the yellow light of her magic—struck his face.

"Lochlan!" He went down like a dead weight.

"Yes. Fear is definitely the right emotion." He groaned as he rolled over in the grass, her bright red palm print on his face. "Take a few deep breaths and focus on the reason for your fear. Try to contain it. Understand it. You can control it better when you understand the source of the emotion."

Lochlan just kissed her. It ignited her anger, but more than that, it terrified her. *Why?* Her magic continued to simmer, and yellow sparks danced around her fingertips. The heat of her magic surprised her, but she was part Eldur—part fire itself, or so it seemed.

"Why does my kiss frighten you?" Lochlan pushed her to explore the emotion.

"I don't know. It was a shock." She brushed her still-tingling lips. She could almost taste his magic—like cinnamon and cloves. Warm and spicy. A second wave of fear spread through her, heightening her magic and fanning the flames.

"Do you truly fear me?" Lochlan sounded almost hurt by the idea.

"No I—" But she did. At least on some level. She didn't believe for a second that he would intentionally hurt her. "I trusted your brother, and look where that got me." The magic moved from just under her skin to deep within her core, simmering there, waiting for her guidance.

Lochlan approached her, taking her hands in his. "For the last time, Brea Robinson, I am not my brother."

"You make me nervous." Brea pulled away from his grasp. "That's all." She didn't like the honesty of her words. She knew in her heart that Lochlan was nothing like Griff.

"I think you fear what Finn would say if he knew I kissed you."

"Uh, confusion much? That's the emotion I'm feeling right now. What are you even talking about?"

"You like Finn."

"Sure, we're friends. Besides, from what I hear, you're the one who likes Finn that way." Her nerves spiked at that admission. Her chest ached with the intensity of her magic as it seeped into her palms.

"That was ages ago."

"How long were you boyfriends?"

"Such a human thing to say." He chuckled.

"We're heading back toward anger and irritation again."

"We weren't exactly together. We were just boys. We

cared a great deal for each other—still do—and we experimented with those feelings. He was my first kiss. Kind of like yours with Myles."

"Wait, what?" How did he know anything about her first kiss?

"Well, I just assumed." Lochlan refused to meet her gaze.

"But how did you know my first kiss was an experiment?" She was nearly fourteen when it happened. She and Myles were out riding his horses and stopped at their favorite spot where their farms met along a babbling brook right beside the tree they always said was theirs. That was the day they decided they wanted to know what all the fuss was about. So they shared a kiss. It was sweet and one of her favorite memories of Myles, but it was also the day they both knew they were a hundred percent just friends.

"Lochlan O'Shea, how long have you been watching me?"

"Years." He turned to meet her gaze, his face revealing nothing.

"Years?"

"At first it was for your mothers. They wanted to know how you were doing. I was fifteen the first time I visited you. You were just a kid then. But you were always with Myles. Your relationship then reminded me of what I'd never had with Griff. It made me miss him."

"And then, what? You kept spying on me?"

"Not spying." He finally met her eyes. "Never spying. I was watching over you, making sure you were safe. Making sure your mothers had news of you—that they could get to know you through me."

"How often?"

"Every few months. Since you were eleven. I mostly saw you at school or just after. I was fascinated with the human education system."

"You watched me for seven years? And you saw our first kiss? Our only kiss?"

"It was then that I realized your relationship with Myles no longer reminded me of what I didn't have with Griff, but what I'd found with Finn. Our first kiss was similar. Just an experiment between the best of friends. Innocent, but no less important."

She should be mad. She should be furious. Brea wiped away the scalding hot tear trailing down her face. Her magic still churned inside her, waiting for an outlet.

"I know you better than you think I do, Brea. You're strong. Look at you. It's your first day, and already you're holding your magic like a natural."

"It's night." Darkness had fallen around them and the orchard glowed under the simmering light of the branches. "Is this normal?" She needed to focus on the lesson and not on the violation of her privacy Lochlan just admitted to. He might not call it spying, but she did.

"No, but you are not normal, Brea. I've suspected it for a long time, but now I know for certain. Please come sit with me." He sank to the ground, patting the grass beside him. Brea reluctantly joined him

"I'm not happy about this news. Just so you know."

"We have bigger things to discuss. It is nightfall, and you still hold your magic. I need to know how it feels. Is it as strong as it was before sunset?"

"No, it has calmed. It's because I dealt with the emotions, right?"

"Partly. Though the moment my magic surfaced at nightfall, yours should have vanished."

"What does that mean?"

"We know your father was of Fargelsi. A royal."

"Regan's brother."

"Did you know he was the rightful king of Gelsi before Regan killed him?"

Brea took a deep breath, the magic still churning in her core, but the heat had cooled in the absence of the sun. "No. I did not know that. It seems there will never be an end to the things people keep from me."

"Most fae in your circumstance would take after their mother's magic. As far as your magic is concerned, you should be Eldurian. But you have your father's magic too."

"I have Eldur magic during the day and Gelsi at night?"

"No. I think you have both at the same time. During the day, your fire magic is present, but it is bolstered by your earth magic, making you incredibly strong."

"Great. So now I'm a magic freak?"

"You're also a royal, whether you like it or not. I know that is not something you're willing to recognize yet.

"My mother is a queen. My crazy aunt is a queen. I am not."

"Royal bloodlines are strong. And you have two of the strongest coursing through your veins."

"So I'm an extra-supersized fae freak?"

Lochlan ignored her. "Between your dual magic, your father's royal blood, and your mothers, you are likely the most powerful fae our world has ever seen. If that ever becomes common knowledge, our people will look to you as a savior. And our enemies..." He didn't need to finish that sentence because they both knew.

Savior.

Fae freak.

Royal.

The labels this world threw at Brea were too much. She couldn't handle the constant expectations, the gobs of information she still didn't know.

And the kiss.

She lay in her bed, staring at the canopy overhead. Too many emotions to decipher rolled through her like waves, bringing her magic to a crest before it tumbled into her stomach, crashing in on itself.

Lochlan tricked her. The kiss was nothing more than him trying to stir up her emotions and get her power to explode out of her. He hadn't done it again in the week they'd been training, but he used other tactics, talking about her family in Ohio and some of the things he'd witnessed. Embarrassment burned through her.

How many times had she told her mom there was someone watching her? On some level, she'd felt it and even seen him, claiming there was a boy with pointed ears and flashing eyes.

All that got her were multiple stays at the Clarkson Institute.

And he'd seen it all. Had he watched them strap her to a bed as she screamed she wasn't lying?

Did he watch when her dad called her every name his drink-addled brain could conjure?

He thought he knew her because he spent all these years watching over her, but she wasn't even sure she knew herself. She knew she should feel creeped out that her mom would send someone to spy on her, a teenager no less, but instead, she took an odd comfort in it. Even when she'd been locked away, she hadn't been alone.

Lochlan wasn't Griff, and maybe it was time for her to stop treating him like they had the same motives. One wanted to manipulate her while the other had devoted his life to keeping her safe.

Kicking off her covers, she sat up as Rowena entered the room carrying a tray that no doubt held Brea's breakfast.

"Morning, Ro."

Rowena set the tray on the table and placed her hands on her hips. "Ro? What have I told you about that silly nickname?"

"You know you love it." Brea's lips curled into a smile. "Or would you prefer Wena? Rowy? Lady Wen?"

"My name is Rowena, my lady."

"Okay, no nicknames for you. Got it." Brea snagged a pastry off the tray and wrapped Rowena in a hug. "Thanks for breakfast."

Rowena stiffened. "My lady, this isn't proper."

Brea laughed. "So?" She released the uncomfortable maid and bounced toward her wardrobe. "I think I'll get my Eldur Brew in the city this morning." She hadn't been into the city in the weeks since Lochlan and Finn returned. Maybe it was finally starting to master her magic or starting to trust this place, but she felt better than she had any day since coming to this world, and probably before.

She flung open the wardrobe doors and flipped through the dresses, wanting something simple. "Rowena, just for today, I'd like to forget about every bad thing that has happened."

"Forgetting does not make it disappear, my Lady."

"Yes, I know that. But I need to smile. Maybe even laugh. I want to have fun." She looked back over her shoulder. "Does fun exist in the fae world?"

Rowena's expression softened. "Yes, Lady Brea, though, it's rare for royals in Eldur."

"Ah, but I'm not an Eldur royal. This city only knows me as a Fargelsian princess."

Rowena stepped to her side and pulled a simple yellow dress free. "This one."

Brea smiled. "You're right. It's perfect." Knowing Rowena wouldn't care because of the odd fae lack of modesty, Brea shed her sleeping gown and slid the sheath dress over her head.

"Sit," Rowena ordered, pointing to the stool in front of the vanity. "Now that you are a known princess, I cannot have you wandering into the city looking like any old commoner." She ran a jeweled brush through Brea's long hair before twisting it into a braid and wrapping it around the crown of her head. "And you are not to go alone. I don't know how your mothers allowed it before."

"They were a little preoccupied, Rowena."

"Yes, well, we all miss Alona, but you're their daughter too, and you deserve their full attention."

Brea turned her smile on Rowena. She was the first person to voice what Brea had been feeling since arriving. Alona being abducted was a tragedy, but she wanted a place in this family too.

She thought back on Lochlan's revelations, and her smile widened. "I have had their attention. My entire life they have cared." That knowledge lifted a weight from her, freeing her from the abandonment she hadn't even realized she'd felt.

Yes, Myles and Alona were still prisoners. Aunt Regan would still come after her if she ever left the safety of Raudur City.

Lochlan was still a frustrating enigma of a man.

But, just once, she wanted to be a young woman

exploring a new world she'd found herself in. No worries, nothing to push her magic out of control.

It was her birthday present to herself, even though that day was past.

She belted the waist of the dress, much to Rowena's dismay, and tied the pouch of coins her mom gave her to the belt. Slipping into her boots, she waved goodbye to Rowena and darted into the hall.

Getting into the city was about more than just having fun. She'd made friends there and was anxious to see them. But Rowena would have a fit if she didn't find an escort.

Maybe Tierney would go with her. Changing direction, she headed toward the throne room. Her two moms were never far from each other's sides. She figured the queen would have duties to attend to, but her wife might enjoy a trip.

The door stood partially open and arguing voices filtered out. Brea recognized Lochlan and Eamon Donovan immediately. She slipped into the back of the room.

"There is nothing we can do about it," the queen stated calmly.

Lochlan ran a hand through his hair. "So, my uncle is allowed to just welcome the prisoners into Iskalt?"

Prisoners?

Eamon held up a hand. "Your Majesty, we have company. Maybe this is a discussion for another time."

All eyes fell on Brea, and she wished she'd just gone into the city on her own.

"Dear." Tierney rushed toward her. "Good morning." Her kind smile relaxed Brea's nerves. "What brings you to the throne room so early?"

"Um... I wanted to see if you'd like to go into the city today."

"Oh, darling, I would love to, but I have appointments most of the day."

"Oh. Okay." Brea's good mood plummeted. "I can just go by myself then. That's not a problem."

"Nonsense." Her face brightened. "Lochlan will take you." She clapped her hands together like it was a grand idea.

Brea looked to Lochlan, who'd jerked his gaze their way upon hearing his name. She'd avoided him outside of training, and his dark look told her he had no interest in going into the city today.

"That's okay. He doesn't have to."

"Nonsense, Brea." She looked to her wife across the room. "Faolan, can you spare Loch for the day?"

Faolan slumped on her throne, looking exhausted despite it being early in the day. "Well, there is little we can do on this matter. Lochlan is all yours."

They traded him like he had no say, but he probably didn't. As a ward of this palace, he probably obeyed the queen in anything.

Lochlan grumbled something under his breath and walked toward the door. "All right, Brea, let's go."

Brea ran after him, struggling to match his pace. "Really,

you don't have to. I know spending time with me isn't high on your priority list."

He stopped walking, not turning to her. "Why would you say such a silly thing?"

She shrugged.

"Brea, we train every afternoon and evening. I'm not the one who has been avoiding you outside of that."

"I haven't—okay, I have. I just feel super weird that you know all these things about me, but also I—"

"Like it."

"Yeah. I mean no. I mean... I don't know. I feel... protected? That's probably not the right word. I know you were only there on orders from the queen, but I like thinking I wasn't alone at some of the worst times."

Lochlan started walking again, still not looking at her. "I was ordered to go to the human world once a year, Brea, but I was there much more than that." His voice was low as if he couldn't believe the words he said.

A smile spread across her face, bringing back the happiness she'd felt in her room earlier. "Okay."

Opting not to have any of the guards fetch horses, they walked down the long road from the palace to the great city beyond. Brea buzzed with excitement the closer they got.

"I know you do not read," Lochlan started. "But I'd like to visit the bookshop while we're here."

"Oh good. I want to see Fiona anyway."

"How do you know Fiona?" He looked sideways at her.

"She's my friend."

His brow creased. "Oh, right. She comes to the palace to

take care of the library. Stay close to me today. This city can be dangerous and is very crowded the closer we get to the market." As they entered the city streets, he pointed out shops and landmarks as if she'd never been there before.

It took her a while to realize he didn't think she had. She bit back a grin and nodded along with his explanations for everything they saw.

Outside his tavern, Xander swept the walkway, his large shoulders hunched forward.

Forgetting Lochlan by her side, Brea shouted, "Xander!"

The burly man looked up, a grin spread across his face. "Well, if it isn't our Fargelsian princess."

She ran across the road, narrowly missing being hit by a cart carrying casks. She threw her arms around Xander, realizing how much she'd missed being with anyone who didn't treat her like a royal.

He laughed and patted her back.

A cough cleared behind them, but Brea ignored Lochlan as someone appeared in the doorway of the tavern.

Adamina squealed when she saw her, and the two girls ran into each other's arms. "It's been weeks." Adamina squeezed her.

"Can't breathe, Mina." Brea laughed as she stepped back from the girl.

"Sir Lochlan." Xander's eyes widened as he finally took notice of Lochlan. "Welcome."

"Xander." Lochlan inclined his head. Of course he'd know the tavern owner.

Leaving the men outside, Adamina pulled Brea through

the door. "I just made some Eldur Brew. It's like I knew I'd get a visit from a princess today."

"Please don't call me that."

Adamina giggled. "Why didn't you tell us? We just thought you were an escaped Fargelsian noble, not the princess."

Brea shrugged and dropped into a chair. "Reasons."

Adamina shook her head and walked back into the kitchen. Xander and Lochlan walked in, both stiff with discomfort. Lochlan had that effect on people.

Brea patted the chair beside her. "Relax. It'll be good for you."

He sat beside her, his eyes traveling over her face. "How is it that the people in this city are so infatuated with you?" He leaned forward, putting his elbows on the table. "I'm not sure you even noticed how many Eldurians waved to us on the way here. They love you. Why?"

"They don't love me," she scoffed. She'd never been the lovable type. In school, the kids made fun of her, despised her.

He sat back, his eyes never leaving her. "What am I missing?"

Adamina returned with two steaming mugs. She set them on the table. "Eldur Brew, coming up."

Brea brought the cup to her lips and inhaled with a sigh. The brew burned her tongue, but she didn't care.

"Eldur Brew?" Lochlan stared at his cup in disgust. "Put it down, Brea. That's not a drink suitable for a princess."

"Don't be such a snob."

He looked too Adamina. "You serve her a commoner's drink?"

Brea set her mug down and stared daggers at him. "Don't be a douche."

"See, I knew it was an insult!"

"Fine. Yes, douchey means obnoxious." She raised a brow. "Offensive."

He met her gaze, his voice dropping. "That is how you see me?"

"Sometimes, yes." She stood, sending an apologetic smile to Adamina and Xander who watched on in fascination.

"What are you doing?" Lochlan asked.

She rounded his chair and put her hands on his shoulders. "Relax, Loch. No one here is watching you or judging you. We aren't surrounded by gilded palace halls. No one here wears a crown." Her hands slid down his arms, and she squeezed. "Now, pick up the drink that Xander and Mina have graciously provided. Take a sip, because drinks do not have class distinctions."

She released him, fully expecting him to shove the mug away like the petulant child he could be. Instead, he lifted it, staring into the dark liquid before tilting the cup against his lips.

Brea moved to stand beside Adamina and they waited in anticipation.

Lochlan set the mug down, a crease between his brows. "That tasted pleasing."

"Pleasing?" Brea yelled. "Seriously? At least tell me I was right?"

He smirked. "I do not think you can handle that."

She laughed. "Well, for your information, my mother enjoys Eldur Brew. Take that for it being a commoner's drink."

His brows shot toward his hairline. "The q—" He caught himself, throwing a look toward the tavern owner and his daughter. "That is quite strange—even for a Fargelsian."

Xander and Adamina joined them at their table until they needed to finish preparations to open for the noonday meal.

By the time Lochlan led Brea back into the street, he'd had three cups of Eldur Brew, but she wouldn't point that out. A small smile played on her lips as she greeted shopkeepers by name. They smiled when they saw her, and a few tried to bow.

Brea spent a lot of time among these people to distract herself from worrying about Lochlan and Finn when they were gone. Now, with Lochlan by her side, it felt more complete. She was still using the city to forget her constant fears, but in that, she and Lochlan were together.

They sauntered through the market, bumping shoulders as the crowd jostled them. "Myles would love this place." She grinned. "So full of life, so vibrant."

"I've never thought of Raudur City in such a way. My duties at the palace and abroad kept me too busy to spend much time dwelling on it."

"Well, maybe you should start. I know you're an Iskalt prince or whatever, but Loch, you grew up here. These people are yours."

"And yours."

She looked away, concealing a smile at the thought. The people of Eldur had a fierce pride in their kingdom, and she was a part of that.

They left the market behind, still walking in step with each other. Brea had waited to ask about what she'd heard, but she couldn't any longer. "What were you arguing about in the throne room this morning?"

"It's not important." He rubbed the back of his neck.

"It sounded important. Something about prisoners."

A sigh pushed past his lips. "Have you been told of the fourth realm of the fae?"

She nodded.

"It is the prison realm, spelled to protect the rest of the fae from its dangers. No one ever escaped... until now. There are now prisoners living in Iskalt, and my uncle has given them places in the army, an army that was an honor to serve when my parents ruled the kingdom. It was the most noble fighting force in all of faedom. Now, it is another in a long line of Iskalt traditions I have to watch my uncle burn to the ground."

Brea glanced down to where his fists clenched at his sides and reached for one of them. She pried his hand open and held onto it for just a moment before releasing him. "I'm sorry. I can't imagine how difficult it is to lose your parents and then your kingdom."

He stopped walking and stared down at her. "My parents died for a noble cause, Brea. I will not take that from them by wishing it was not so." She wanted to ask if that noble cause was her, but held the question back, unsure if the answer would hurt her more or help her understand.

Lochlan continued. "One day, I will reclaim what is rightfully mine. And then you and I can repair the damage that has been wrought on our world." He turned to walk into the bookshop.

Brea ran after him. "Me? What do I have to do with it?"

He froze inside the door. "You, Brea Robinson, will be the queen of Eldur."

Her jaw dropped open, and the magic froze in her veins, threatening to shatter her like an icicle crashing into the ground. Queen? No. That wasn't the deal. "But I don't even want to be a princess," she whispered.

Before she got a chance to ask any questions, Fiona swept in, brushing right by Lochlan to wrap Brea in a hug. "Lochlan O'Shea, what did you do to the girl? She looks as white as an Iskalt winter."

He shrugged as if he truly had no idea why she suddenly couldn't speak. Fear, but also anger, curled inside her, but she breathed deeply, using the mental exercises Lochlan taught her to control the emotions—and therefor control the magic. It did no one any good if she wrecked Fiona's shop.

"You're okay, dear." Fiona rubbed her back as she guided her farther into the store.

She should have known Eldur wanted her for the same reason as Fargelsi. They needed an heir, one with magic. It made so much sense. Alona couldn't inherit the throne because she had no power, hadn't they told her that a few times already? How had she not put it together?

Faolan didn't want to bring her daughter back to get to know her. She needed Brea the same way Regan had.

Brea's breaths came in short gasps as she did everything she could to control her magic.

"Lochlan," Fiona hissed. "What happened?"

"I told her something she didn't want to hear." He sounded so nonchalant as if he hadn't just pulled a "you're a wizard, Harry" on her. Only, she already knew about the magic. She wasn't just a wizard. More like a wizard-queen.

How ridiculous was that?

Her magic snapped inside her as she gained full control and marched toward where Lochlan thumbed through books on a shelf.

Pushing her hand out in front of her, she forced Lochlan against the shelf. It rattled from the impact, and a book teetered before falling on him. He tried to pick it up.

"Don't move," she growled.

"Calm down, Brea. Rein in the magic. Control the emotions."

Her jaw clenched. "I am controlling it, and I don't want to rein it in. You listen to me, Lochlan O'Shea. I am no one's pawn. You fae-people watch me my entire life after abandoning me to a world I didn't belong in. You trade me between kingdoms like a prize. I might have Fargelsian royal blood and Eldurian royal blood, but I am still Brea Robinson of Ohio. And I will make my own blasted choices."

He nodded, his eyes never leaving hers. "You're going to make an amazing fire queen."

Pulling her magic back in, she released him and turned

before striding out the door. It wasn't Lochlan's fault people kept things from her, or that she was in this situation in the first place. If it wasn't for him, she doubted anyone would be honest with her.

No, there was someone else who needed to hear what she had to say.

"I am not a queen." Brea crashed into the throne room, holding her magic back and using her brute strength instead. Okay, she ordered a guard to use his strength and stared him down until he obeyed.

Now, said guard stood cowering near the door while Brea stomped down the long aisle to her mother's gilded throne. A throne she refused to sit on at any point in the future.

Her mother looked up from the Eldurian citizen she'd been speaking to--an older woman who set a basket of eggs at the queen's feet. It was an image straight out of a novel where some fantasy queen accepted gifts from her people as they entreated her to settle land disputes and other issues.

Somehow, it seemed almost beneath the great Queen

Faolan. Brea only saw her interact with the people at her birthday party, but this was... different.

"Princess Brea of Fargelsi." Her mother's voice was a cold reminder to keep her mouth shut as she gestured to the citizens waiting along the far wall. "Please, tell me what has happened that is more important than this woman's missing child."

Brea's anger simmered and faded as she took in the haggard faces around the room. To the queen's right stood Captain Donovan, his warm gaze setting her at ease.

The doors to the throne room opened again, and Lochlan rushed in with Finn following close behind.

"I'm sorry, your Majesty." Lochlan bowed. "I could not stop her."

Queen Faolan—because she was a queen at the moment and not a mother—studied Brea, her eyes narrowed. "Captain Donovan, take the Gelsian princess to my rooms. She can await me there while I finish my service to these fine people."

How could she all at once sound like a dragon queen and a fair and noble ruler? A shiver raced down Brea's spine, and she pushed out a breath. She was better than barging into throne rooms and stomping through palaces. That wasn't the girl she wanted to be—a spoiled princess, upset when she didn't get her way. The true Brea Robinson knew what hard work felt like, how it was when she had to stand tall when the whole world was against her.

Turning on her heel, she lifted her chin and followed the

captain, not sparing a glance for Lochlan or Finn who tried to follow.

"Lochlan, Finn," the queen's voice rang out behind her. "You two must stay here. The princess will survive without your yammering."

By the time they reached the queen's rooms, a deep weariness replaced the anger inside Brea. She smiled a thank you at the captain before he left her in the queen's sitting room.

Silence surrounded her, and she walked to the floor to ceiling windows that looked out over the city, a city she wanted to call her own. She loved the people, the shops, the life. But it wasn't hers.

Eldur wanted her for the same reason Fargelsi had, the crown. How could she be an heir to two kingdoms when she didn't want one? All she wished for was a family who cared about her and a home that felt like hers.

What had she gotten instead?

Parents who abandoned her in another world. A palace she'd never truly belong in. And people who wanted her for nothing more than the royal blood in her veins.

Just perfect.

Glancing down at her long dress, she tried to brush the dirt from the bottom of it. That's what she got for running through the city streets to confront the queen.

Her eyes flicked from her mother's pristine white couch to the dirty dress. No, she couldn't sit there no matter how tired she was.

Instead, she slid to the floor in front of the window,

remembering how she'd once imagined Eldur as a cruel place full of dragons and other creatures. Other than her mother's sometimes coldness, it was more than she could have imagined. If she refused the crown, would she be sent away?

She didn't know how long she'd been sitting there when the door opened, revealing the immaculate queen, her eyes sweeping the room.

"Brea?" She craned her neck to see into the other room.

"Here." Brea lifted a hand to get her mother's attention.

"What on earth are you doing on the floor?"

Brea climbed to her feet. "I didn't want to dirty your couch."

"Couch? Oh, you mean the settee? Darling, you are a princess. My people might not know the truth of which kingdom you call your own, but an Eldurian princess never sits on the floor." She lowered herself to the couch, er, settee and patted the spot beside her. "Come now. I know you think us very primitive, but do you honestly think this has never been dirtied? We have magic, Brea."

"You... Clean with your magic?"

"Heavens no." She put a hand to her chest. "But the palace maids do. Lochlan and Alona used to have quite the fondness for mud, so it was a good thing."

Brea smiled at the image of a little boy and girl running to her stiff mother caked with mud. She sat next to her mother and tapped one finger against her knee.

"So," Faolan began. "Lochlan has told you."

"That I'm... That I'm..." She couldn't say it.

"Going to be queen?"

Brea nodded. "That."

"Well, what did you think would happen? We've already told you of Alona's inability to inherit due to her lack of magic."

"What about Lochlan?"

"He is not my son. And besides, he has his own kingdom to rule once he is strong enough to deal with that wretched uncle of his." She pursed her lips. "Why does this distress you?"

Brea looked away. "I don't know how long I've been in the Fae world, but it can't have been more than six months. Until then, I thought I was a human farm girl. I'm not..." What was she going to say? She wasn't good enough? That she'd fail and let everyone down? "Don't fae live longer than humans? You will be queen for a long time."

She smiled sadly. "Brea, I have been the queen of Eldur for one hundred and forty seven years."

Brea's mouth fell open, but she had no words.

"I was eight when my mother died, leaving me the crown. Do you think I was ready for it then? The truth is I am tired. I have seen many wars and political battles."

"Is that why you sent Loch to find me in the human realm?"

She shook her head. "I have wanted to bring you home every day since I handed you over to my greatest friends."

"Loch's parents?"

"Yes. They took you to the human realm and lost their lives for it. You need to understand something about this world, Brea. Nothing is done without a reason, a purpose. In the noble households, every child is conceived to fill a role. A royal line is only as strong as it's succession."

"So, you're saying you found someone to have a child with in hopes that child could rule one day?"

She nodded. "But that is not all. Regan of Fargelsi had begun to rise in power. Her magic was much stronger than mine—which is not supposed to be possible. Eldur is always the stronger power of the two, evened only by Fargelsians' ability to use magic without the sun. We were scared of her, to be honest."

"We?" Brea froze. "You mean you and Regan's brother, my father."

"Your father..." A smile tilted her lips. "He was a great man, a great king of Fargelsi. We could see the future unfolding. Regan's power would only grow, so we needed a weapon, someone who could use their power both night and day, but hold all the strength of Eldurian blood."

Brea leaned forward, resting her elbows on her knees as she hung her head. "Me." She was a weapon of mass destruction, only brought to life for that purpose.

"Yes." Her mother's voice was no more than a whisper now. "Brandon and I conceived a child. It was our duty to this world. Regan killed him before you were born. She knew what we'd done, but she couldn't get to me here in Eldur. It was clear to her right away Alona was not the child of our union, but you were gone, safely kept in the most nondescript place we could find in the human world."

A laugh burst free of Brea. "You could say that about Ohio." She rubbed her face before lifting her eyes to her mother's. "So, you're saying I have no choice, that I never have. I still don't know who I am or who I trust. How am I supposed to be a queen?"

Her mother reached out and took her hand. "I will teach you, dear. I'm not relinquishing the crown tomorrow. And as for who you are—you're my daughter, and I'm so very glad you are finally home."

Tears blurred Brea's vision, and she tried to wipe them away, but her mother wouldn't let go of her hand. "But I'm not Alona. You don't even know me."

"A mother does not have to know her child to love them. Alona is in my heart. She might not be of my blood, but I love her no differently from you. Not a second goes by where she is not in my thoughts, my fears. Sometimes I can't breathe when I think how far away she is, how in danger." She wiped a thumb under Brea's eye. "But I have experienced that same fear every day for eighteen years as I've been missing you. Alona never replaced you, the same as you cannot replace her. There is room for both of you in here." She placed a hand over her heart.

Brea shot to her feet as tears continued to cascade down her cheeks. "I need some space." She pulled her hand free, not watching to see if her mother's expression fell.

"Yes." The queen stood and flattened the crease out of her dress. "I expect you do. Take your time, Brea. Just remember, you are fae. You have as much responsibility to this world as I did when I made my decisions."

Rushing toward the door, Brea pulled it open and sprinted past the guards. Tears clogged in her throat, and the only sound was her footsteps echoing against the stone floors.

She reached the courtyard with the naked-man fountain and collapsed against the low stone wall circling it. Digging in the pouch at her waist, she pulled out every coin she had and started tossing them in one by one.

"I wish this was all a dream."

"I wish I could just have one more day on Myles' farm under our tree."

"I wish this stupid magic didn't threaten to boil over every time I got emotional."

"I wish I was normal."

That's what she'd wanted her entire life, wasn't it? To be normal? For the hallucinations and energy underneath her skin to just go away. And now... She was born for one specific purpose: to be a weapon against her aunt.

She wanted to kill Regan for bringing Myles into this, for taking Alona from Finn and their mothers. But could she?

If she allowed herself to become this... magical bullet or whatever it was they wanted her to be, would she ever be anything else?

Lochlan was probably never going to sleep again.

Not with Brea Robinson's voice in his head.

"I wish this was all a dream."

She hadn't known he'd followed her to the courtyard or that he'd watched her just like so many times before. Not talking or revealing his presence. Only listening, seeing.

And what he'd seen was a girl who didn't want to be here. She didn't see how much she truly belonged, how the people reacted to her.

How Lochlan reacted to her.

The first time he'd wanted to reach out to her instead of just watching in the human realm was when he was seventeen years old. He'd walked across the barren fields stretching in front of the Robinson's house. Paint curled and peeled from the worn wooden walls. A tire swing hung from the large oak in the yard, but it looked like the rope would break with the tiniest weight.

And there stood a girl in the barn entrance, her hair streaming out behind her. He'd seen her a hundred times before as he kept watch for the Eldurian queen. This girl in ripped pants and a shirt so old the colors had faded from the fabric... She was a princess.

Most of the time he saw her with Myles, but not this time. He'd watched much closer than the queen would have allowed because he had to know what she was doing.

Music had filtered from their dilapidated barn, and he'd peered through a broken window to find Brea dancing as if she'd never heard a beat in her life. He'd shrank back into the shadows when Myles finally joined her.

"What are you doing?" Myles had yelled over the music.

A grin lit up the sad girl's face, reaching all the way to her eyes. "It's my birthday, Myles, and I'm throwing myself a party."

Lochlan hadn't stayed long enough to see if Myles brought a gift. He'd run back across the fields, using the night to hide him as he forced open a portal into Eldur and barreled through, landing right in the middle of a royal celebration. Time was different in the fae realm—the seasons here never aligned with the human realm. Alona's birthday was more than two months ago for them, but there was always a royal celebration on this day every year.

He'd gone from a lonely girl the world seemed to have ignored and her joyful party for two to a ball fit for a princess. He only now realized that yearly ball was meant for the absent Eldurian Princess.

He'd never been the same after that day. Nothing had. He told the queen what he always did, that Brea was safe and healthy, never mentioning the other h word that would have been a lie. She smiled sometimes, but Brea was never truly happy.

And he certainly didn't mention he'd become fascinated with a girl he'd never spoken to, one who didn't know their world existed. As Brea grew older, he realized somewhere through the years, he'd fallen in love with her.

Lochlan sighed as he rolled over in bed, the blankets twisting about his legs. She drove him crazy, but he'd thought he'd gotten over his teenage crush a long time ago.

Then he heard her say she wished none of this was real, and it sent a spear right through his heart. He was real. His world wasn't a dream. She had to get used to that.

He rubbed his face, remembering her horror at the thought of being queen. Hadn't he had those same fears about one day ruling Iskalt? Maybe they had more in common than he'd thought, but he could never admit to the terror thrumming through him at the mention of finally taking the crown from his uncle.

Lochlan might never be able to tell Brea how he felt those years ago. There might be no hope for them, but they'd rule this world together one day as allies and maybe even friends.

A knock sounded on his door, and he glanced to the

window. The world outside was still dark, and he couldn't fathom who would be calling at such an hour.

"Just a moment," he called. Slipping from his bed, he reached for the silk robe on a peg by the armoire and shrugged it on, tying it at the waist.

The knock echoed through the room once more before the door burst open, revealing a heaving Finn.

"What's wrong?" Lochlan had always been able to read every emotion in his best friend's face.

"You must come. I was on duty tonight, and we've received a messenger."

"That seems like information for the queen." He raised an eyebrow.

Finn shook his head. "This man... He comes from Iskalt."

Ice shot through Lochlan's veins, and he was sure his eyes frosted over as his magic thrummed to life. Nothing good came out of Iskalt. Not anymore. He stepped into his boots, not bothering to lace them up or get dressed. "Has the queen been informed?"

"Yes. My father went to fetch her."

Lochlan grunted. "Don't let Faolan hear you say anyone fetched her. Come, I must see this messenger."

Finn's brow creased. "You're not going to change?"

"No." Where Iskalt was involved, Lochlan wanted to be the first to know. It might have been a selfish need, being that the queen deserved that right in her own palace, but Lochlan had never been able to shake the guilt over letting his cruel uncle rule Iskalt for so many years.

Finn led him to the great hall where they'd let the

messenger warm himself with an ale by the fire. "He rode for many days, only stopping to change horses. I don't think he has slept since leaving Iskalt."

Lochlan gripped Finn's shoulder. "Thank you. Can you send for Brea? I have a hunch I'm going to need her to hear this."

Finn nodded and sent someone to wake Brea while Lochlan crossed the hall to where the hearth breathed life into the cold room. The orange glow reflected off the face of an older man with gray hair tied into a knot on top of his head. His haggard face basked in the warmth as icy eyes stared into the flames.

He wrapped both hands around his mug and lifted it to his lips.

"What is your name, sir?" Lochlan stopped beside the man's chair and looked down at him.

The old man lifted his tired eyes. "Duff O'Dell, your Highness."

"I'm not—"

"I know who you are. I'd recognize those eyes anywhere, sire."

Lochlan turned a wooden chair and sat facing the man. "You are from Iskalt?"

He took another sip of ale before setting the empty mug on the table next to him. "You do not remember me."

"Should I?"

"No. You were a child when I served your parents. I was one of their personal guards."

"Do you serve my uncle?"

Duff sighed. "We all serve your uncle, sire. I no longer guard the king, but my son does. We've expected our princes to come home for many years, and you never have."

"I—"

"No need to explain it to me, boyo. Most of Iskalt is under the thrall of Callum O'Shea. They will follow him to death, but only because they think they have no other option."

Lochlan clenched his jaw. "And you?"

"I have had the truth of the man revealed. It is why I have come, risking my family back in Iskalt."

Lochlan was about to tell him to speak when commotion sounded behind them. The queen's arrival. Faolan breezed into the room with no care of who her retinue disturbed. Few others lingered besides Lochlan and Duff, but the queen's guards and maids turned the quiet conversation into a crowded state report. He breathed a sigh of relief when Brea slipped in at the back of the group, doing her best to go unseen.

"Lochlan." Faolan held chastisement in her eyes. "You are not to speak to messengers without me."

"Dear." Tierney put a hand on her arm. "If this has to do with his kingdom, he has the right."

Faolan's gaze softened when she looked at her wife. "Yes. It is late, so let's see what has gotten us all out of our beds." One of her guards dragged a wingback chair to them, and the queen sat.

"Your Majesty." Lochlan dipped his head. "This is Duff O'Dell. He has come with news from Iskalt."

"If you'll excuse me, my Lady." Those nearby sucked in their breath at the term. Lochlan closed his eyes for a brief moment, but the queen didn't correct her title. "Lochlan O'Shea is my ruler, not an Eldurian queen. I came to speak with him."

"And here we both sit." Faolan looked wholly unaffected. "Tell us why you have come."

"There are too many ears," Duff hissed.

The queen sighed. "Leave us," she ordered. "Eamon, Finn, Brea, you stay." The guards and servants hurried out, leaving the cavernous room empty except their small group.

Duff focused his gaze on Lochlan, ignoring the queen and the rest. "I live in a village about a day's ride from the Vatlands between Iskalt and Eldur. We are a quiet village, peaceful. Until now. We've been finding friends and neighbors dead. At first, we thought a sickness had come, but there are marks on the bodies, burns. They have rings of charred flesh crossing their torsos."

"A barrier spell," Lochlan whispered. He'd seen those kinds of burns before while stationed along the Fargelsian border. Anyone with full Fargelsian blood died if they tried to cross.

"A barrier spell, your Majesty?" Duff looked to him in confusion.

Lochlan leaned forward. "Tell me, Mr. O'Dell, do people still travel to your village? For trade and other purposes?"

Duff nodded. "Yes. Though, the flow of traders to the markets has slowed."

"Then it is not complete yet."

"Lochlan," Queen Faolan snapped. "What you speak of is not possible. Callum O'Shea does not have the power for a barrier spell."

"Don't you see, your Majesty? He's crafting it, or at least trying to, using one of his own villages as the test before expanding it to all of Iskalt, turning the people into prisoners just like those in Fargelsi."

"But how? It would take more than Iskalt magic for a spell of such magnitude. And it doesn't explain how trade has not stopped."

"But it does." Lochlan tried to remember everything he'd learned studying the Fargelsi barrier. "It takes an enormous amount of power to sustain even a small barrier around a village. More power than Callum can wield on his own. My uncle has never been a great magician. As he tries to complete the barrier, his magic seeps into the village. It's not complete yet, but it is killing people all the same."

Queen Faolan covered her mouth with her hand. "He doesn't have that kind of power."

"Regan does." Brea's voice surprised Lochlan, and he sat up straighter.

He met Brea's eyes. "Speak."

Brea bit her lip. "Fargelsi and Iskalt have an... understanding. I don't know if that's the right word. To them, Eldur is the common enemy. A horrific spell such as this has to come from my aunt. She'd help your uncle. I'm sure of it."

"Even so," Queen Faolan started. "There is nothing we can do. Iskalt problems are not our own."

Lochlan hardly heard her. He barely noticed her bidding

goodnight to the messenger, or Duff looking to him helplessly as a maid led him to a room for the night.

All Lochlan could see was Brea, and the secrets she'd kept.

A secret that could end them all.

Lochlan needed to find his bed again to try to obtain the elusive sleep. Maybe then he'd receive some clarity.

Some answers.

But he'd never claimed to do the smart thing.

"Loch," Finn called him back, but Lochlan brushed past him on his way out the door.

He needed to speak to Brea. He only planned to ask questions, to find out the whole truth. Her mother refused to help Iskalt, but it was his kingdom and he'd do what he could.

But that was logical Lochlan, and all logic left him the moment he learned what his uncle was doing to their people.

Brea reached her rooms and stopped with her hand on the door. "I know you're following me."

"We need to talk," he growled.

"Fine." She pushed open her door. "By all means come berate me in the middle of the night. I haven't had enough people lecturing me lately."

He didn't miss the sarcasm in her voice, but he also didn't care. There were two Lochlan O'Sheas. One was stuck as a teenage boy wanting to protect the princess and experience just one of her smiles.

The other, the cold Iskalt prince, he'd do anything necessary to get answers.

The latter won out as he kicked the door shut and advanced on Brea. Her eyes flashed yellow as she stood her ground, refusing to move.

"My uncle." His jaw clenched. "Tell me everything."

She crossed her arms. "Only if you back up."

With a sigh, he did as she asked.

She nodded in approval. "I really don't know much. It's not like my aunt let me into important meetings, and everything Griff told me was a lie."

A growl rumbled low in his throat at the mention of his brother and the thought of them together. "Tell me what the Iskalt delegation did after I left Fargelsi."

She shrugged. "Honestly, I don't know. I was kept away from many of the state dinners because I'm a bumbling fool, and my aunt was embarrassed of me."

He took a step toward her, wanting to erase the self-conscious flicker of doubt across her face. "You are no fool, Brea Robinson."

She stepped back, pressing her back against the wall. "I—"

"Is it true?" His voice lowered. "Regan and Callum have formed an alliance?"

"Yes."

"You should have told us the moment we brought you to the palace."

She pushed at his chest. "Oh, you mean when you were all mourning Alona? Or when you left for weeks with no word, leaving us scared out of our minds that something happened to you too?"

She was scared for him? He lifted a hand, planning to cup her cheek. Instead, he gripped her chin and forced it up as he hovered over her. "This was important, Brea."

She hit his hand away. "How was I to know? I've lived my life in the human realm, not this messed up fantasy sideshow. I. Am. Not. One. Of. You."

He leaned down to look into her eyes, his power meeting hers. "You are. You always have been."

"Maybe I don't want to be," she whispered.

He wanted to kiss her. More than anything else in the world, he wanted to feel her lips against his again. But the next time he kissed her, it would be real. He wouldn't be trying to enrage her to fuel her magic. And it wouldn't be a result of this heated anger between them either.

When he kissed her, she would feel in one moment everything he'd bottled up over the years of watching her in the human realm. All the sadness and the pride. Even the tiny bits of joy he'd watch her capture. She'd feel dancing in an abandoned barn and sitting under a gorgeous tree with blue skies overhead.

That was how he once saw her.

And now? The princess of two kingdoms who'd escaped an impenetrable palace and made the population of the entire capital fall in love with her.

"You infuriate me," she said, staring into his eyes, unflinching.

"Not as much as you infuriate me." He stayed where he was, his chest pressed against hers, for a moment longer before reminding himself why he'd come.

Something was happening in Iskalt, something terrible and dangerous.

He took a step back, giving them both space to breathe. "It's time I help my people." All these years he'd been safe in Eldur while they suffered under Callum. "I've abandoned them long enough."

"My mother won't allow it if she thinks it's not Eldur's problem." Brea pushed away from the wall, the yellow fading from her eyes.

Lochlan rubbed the back of his neck. Brea wasn't wrong, but maybe that didn't matter. "I love Faolan like she is my own mother, but she is the queen of Eldur. Iskalt blood runs through my veins, and it's time I let that guide me."

Brea's lips twitched into a smile. "I feel like I'm watching a little boy become a man right before my eyes."

The scowl he unleashed on her had no venom behind it. "I know it must be a foreign concept in the human world,

Brea, but you do not need to voice every thought that comes into your mind."

"So, I guess I shouldn't tell you I'm proud of you for choosing your people over my mother's wishes?"

He turned away from her to hide his smile. "Pride is a useless emotion." In three strides, he reached the door and opened it. As he stepped into the hall, he heard Brea calling behind him.

"I'm proud of my little silk-robe wearing princeling, and I don't care how useless that is."

He shut the door and shook his head with a laugh, his chest expanding with Brea's pride. It may have served no purpose, but he felt her words in every bone of his body.

He glanced down at the robe he'd forgotten he was wearing, and a flush crept up his neck.

Even in his embarrassment, the moment he lay down and set his head against his soft pillow, he fell fast asleep, Brea's pride like a blanket protecting him from the troubles the next days would bring.

"I won't allow it, Lochlan." Queen Faolan perched on her throne in the empty throne room. It was barely light out, but Lochlan had called them all here to discuss the threat on Iskalt.

Brea wasn't sure why she was there. Yawning, she perused the morning buffet, sad to see the absence of Eldur Brew. No matter the time of day, the throne room spread offered the best food to be had in all of Eldur. "Ooh jelly popovers." She helped herself to several of her favorite pastries, wondering if she just went back to bed if anyone would miss her.

"It is none of our business." Shocked, Brea's attention turned to the queen. How could she say such a thing to Loch, knowing how he felt about his people and his absence all these years? It occurred to her that her mother might not know him as well as she thought if she expected him to sit back and watch his uncle turn Iskalt into another Gelsi prison.

"It is my business, your Majesty. I cannot allow my people to suffer any more than I could stand by idly while the people of Eldur suffered. I will leave for Iskalt today, with or without your help. I have nothing but the deepest of respect for you. You have been the mother I've needed all these years—and you always will be—but I can no longer turn a blind eye on my kingdom."

"And what about Alona?" Faolan asked. "Our forces are working hard to bring the Gelsi barrier down. We have to focus on bringing her home, Lochlan. I would have you and Finn stay close to act the moment we receive word the barrier is breaking."

"That's not fair," Brea interjected, a popover halfway to her mouth. "You can't ... take the Iskalt blood from his veins any more than you can give him fire magic. So how can you sit there and tell Lochlan to ignore the suffering of those he feels responsible for?"

"You overstep, Brea." Faolan frowned. "This does not concern you. I don't even know why you were summoned at this early hour. Go back to bed, darling."

"No." Brea met Lochlan's pleading gaze. This was why he'd asked Rowena to send her to the throne room. Only Brea with her human nonsense would have the gall to speak to the queen in such a way. "I mean no disrespect, your Majesty, but if you were a guest in Iskalt and learned your people were being slaughtered here in Eldur, would you ignore it?"

"Of course not, I am queen."

"And Lochlan is their rightful king. He isn't a child anymore, as much as you might like to think of him as the son you never had. Please, don't ask him to choose between you and Alona who are his family, and his people who are his duty. It's cruel." Brea took a step back, thinking she'd pushed her mother too far. "I mean, respectfully, your Majesty." She bobbed a curtsy for added measure.

"She is right," Lochlan said. "I will leave for Iskalt today, but I would prefer if I had your blessing, if not your help."

"I would sooner see you safe at home, here in the palace." Faolan sighed. "But I know the weight of the responsibility you shoulder, Lochlan. I cannot become directly involved in the unrest within Iskalt. I will not require my troops to join you, but you may ask for volunteers. That is the best I can do for you, my son. Please do what you must and return home to us safely." Faolan stood to dismiss them.

"I volunteer as tribute!" Brea stepped toward her mother's throne.

"What?" Faolan looked at her like she might never understand her daughter.

"No." Lochlan looked at her like he might throttle her on the spot.

"You need me." Brea lifted her chin in defiance. "I have fire magic. You'll need me during the day when your magic is dormant."

"I have Finn for that." Lochlan crossed his arms over his

chest. A fleeting emotion showed in his dark blue eyes, but it was gone before Brea could decipher it.

"So, you're going to march into Iskalt—a land where everyone uses magic at night, with a bunch of useless troops —and Finn—who can only use magic during the day?

"Hey." Finn scowled at her. "I think that was an insult."

"If you have to think about it, it was." Brea left her half-eaten popovers on the table. "You need me, Lochlan. I don't have a time limit on my magic."

"You know, she's probably right." Finn shrugged. "She's not trained, but she's better than nothing."

"Hey! I can do stuff." At the very least she could scare people with her erratic magic.

Finn raised a brow as if to say he could give as good as he got.

"No. End of discussion." Lochlan turned toward the queen and gave a curt bow. "Thank you, your Majesty. I will keep you updated with our findings in Iskalt. Finn, we leave before noon."

"I'll be ready." Finn gave Brea a half-hearted shrug, snagging one of her popovers on his way out.

"Try to get some sleep, Brea, darling," her mother said. "It's still much too early to have bothered you with this unfortunate business."

"It's okay. I prefer it when people keep me in the loop with what's happening around us." Brea loaded up her plate with pastries and headed back to her room. She had some packing to do.

"If you are going to steal one of her Majesty's horses, at least steal a good one."

Brea whirled around, cursing herself for making too much noise. "Master Arturo, I uh—didn't want to er—take a horse you might miss."

"I take it you've a mind to follow Master Lochlan and his troops?" Arturo moved to unfasten the saddle she'd just settled onto her mount. An aging mare with a feisty temper if not much speed. "You'll need to move faster than old Red here can manage. You'll take Sassa. She'll get you where you need to go in a hurry."

"Thank you, Master Arturo." She helped move her saddle bags to the young white mare, eager to put as much distance between her and the palace as possible. Brea couldn't put a name to the feeling. She just knew she had do something to help, something that wouldn't make her feel so useless all the time.

"Take the north road, and you should catch them before nightfall. They'll make camp at the plains just south of Loch Sol."

"Don't tell—"

"I never saw you." Arturo smiled, slapping Sassa's rump and setting Brea off along the trail up to the orchard where she'd find the north road. "Don't get lost, my Lady."

"Thank you!" Brea called over her shoulder. It felt good to let Sassa set the pace as they raced through the orchard.

Lochlan and Finn left more than an hour ago, and she had a lot of ground to cover if she was going to catch up to them.

Lochlan spent the morning asking for volunteers and managed to gather a troop of three hundred Eldurian soldiers to accompany him into Iskalt. If he'd taken an extra day or two to plan, he probably could have left with twice that. It made Brea nervous to think of what might lay in wait for him in Iskalt. For all they knew, this whole thing with the dead villagers might be a trap, and he was walking right into it.

"Come on, girl. Let's see what you can do." Brea urged her mount into a full gallop once she reached the north road. A column of dust rose into the sky along the horizon. That cloud was her destination.

An hour into her trip, Brea was convinced the sun was going to kill her. The dry dessert air parched her throat, but she had precious little water with her. Just enough to get her to Loch Sol.

At the top of the rocky rise, Brea hoped she'd find some sign of shade where she could rest and give Sassa a drink of water.

"What are you doing, woman? Are you trying to make me crazy?"

Brea closed her eyes at the sound of his voice. "How did you know I was following you?"

"You kicked up more dust than three hundred soldiers. I figured it was you, or Faolan found some more volunteers for me." Lochlan stood from his seat among a scattering of boulders at the bottom of the hill she'd just crested.

"And which one of those is your preference?" She guided her horse over to his.

"A few hundred soldiers, or one inept girl with erratic magic? Hard choice."

"I won't go back." Brea took a sip from her canteen. "You might as well face it, I'm coming with.

"Just try to stay out of trouble."

"Who me? Contrary to what you might think, I am not a trouble magnet."

Lochlan guided his horse away from hers.

"What are you doing?"

"Moving away from the lightning that is sure to strike you at any second."

"Oh my gosh, this is heaven. Loch, you gotta try this." Brea's voice drifted to him in the darkness. They'd ridden hard all afternoon and reached the hot springs near Loch Sol just as the sun began to set.

He'd sent scouts ahead with orders to make camp near the mud springs Loch Sol was famous for. Judging by the sounds Brea was making, it was worth the extra effort to find the springs. But his mind wasn't on Loch Sol or even Brea who occupied his thoughts often of late. It was with his people.

"Seriously. This is like heaven."

Something warm splattered across his back. "Did you just fling mud at me?"

"Yes. You should try relaxing. Brooding about your

people now when you can't help them yet isn't doing you any good."

"Are you suggesting I join you?"

"Are you suggesting there is something improper about that? I have clothes on in here you know."

"That's not how you're supposed to do it, Brea." He chuckled at her modesty.

"Well, that's how I do it. I don't relish getting mud all up in my lady bits."

Lochlan snorted as he stood and shed his travel stained shirt and trousers, leaving his underthings on. She was right—in her way—worrying wouldn't get him there any faster. Sinking down into the hot mud, Lochlan stifled a groan.

"You could make a fortune selling this stuff to humans." Brea slathered the mud over her shoulders, rubbing it into her tired muscles.

"Eldurians pay a handsome price for this mud. It has healing properties that keep the effects of aging at bay for a time."

"Humans would kill for this stuff."

"Humans are vain creatures." Lochlan settled back into the mud, feeling the tension ease from his shoulders.

"Not all of us are caught up in our looks."

"You aren't human, Brea," he said softly, watching her profile in the darkness.

"Maybe not in body. But in spirit, I think I always will be."

Lochlan moved closer to her, unable to keep his distance.

She had a way of making him feel better even when it seemed his world was falling down around him.

"It's part of your charm. Don't ever lose it, Brea."

"My mother expects me to."

"Give her time. Faolan is a good mother, but she is also very stubborn. I imagine that is where you get it from."

"What kinds of things did you tell my mothers about me after your spying visits?"

Lochlan frowned. He didn't like to think about Brea's life before. The parents who should have adored her, treated her like trash. Alona's biological parents. He could never see much of her in them. They didn't deserve either daughter. "Lots of things. I told them about your school. About Myles. How you loved your horses when you were young and were sad when your parents had to sell them."

"What about all the other stuff?" Her voice was small in the darkness. It stirred something inside him, knowing all she went through in the human world. So many times he'd wanted to bring her home, but it wasn't safe for her then and probably never would be.

"I told your mothers you had nice parents who cared for you as best they could given their limited means."

"Thank you." She stood, letting the mud slide down her body.

"For what?" He joined her, resisting the urge to pull her close.

"For keeping my secrets."

"If I could have changed anything for you, I would have." He took her hand, helping her out of the mud spring.

"Wait, now what?" Brea looked down at herself with a frown.

"Now we walk to the hot springs." He pointed across the sparse forest of stunted trees to the clear waters of one of the many hot springs surrounding Loch Sol. Still holding her hand, he led the way.

"There should be a spa hotel here. I'd never leave." Brea sighed into the cool evening breeze.

"The area around Loch Sol isn't a suitable habitat. It's much too hot during the day, and nothing grows here. But I'm sure if you ask your mother, she would bring wagonloads of the mud into the palace and build a mud spring just for you."

"Here we are. Be careful, Brea, it's very hot." Lochlan reluctantly released her hand as she stepped into the natural sulfur spring to rinse the volcanic mud off.

"It can never be too hot." She tiptoed into the deeper side of the pool, the steam curling the stray locks of her hair falling from the messy knot on top of her head. "I loved taking bubble baths when I was a kid, but my mom rarely let me indulge. Said I made too much of a mess and it cost too much to fill the tub. It was never hot enough or deep enough. And now I have a swimming-pool-sized tub in my bathroom and servants to fill it."

She sounded so sad, like maybe she missed the drunken fools who were supposed to be her parents.

"Do you miss your home?"

"I don't have a home, Loch." She shrugged, dipping her

shoulders under the water, rinsing the mud from her underclothes she'd insisted on wearing into the spring.

"Eldur is your home."

"Maybe some day. It still doesn't feel like it though. I love the city and the people. I'm just not so sure about the palace or those who reside there."

He knew she was still upset about the prospect of becoming queen someday, but that day was likely a distant future where Brea had found her role within her family and the people who already adored her.

"Make yourself useful." He turned his back to her, changing the subject. "Help me wash the mud off where I can't reach."

Her hands felt nice against his hot skin as she rinsed the last of the mud away. "There, that's better." She turned him toward her, running her hands along his arms. "See, relaxing isn't so hard. Even you can do it when you try." She looked up at him with her crooked half smile.

For once, not overthinking his actions, Loch, pulled her close, his hands settling around her as his lips brushed hers. A gasp of surprise escaped her as she tilted her head back to look at him, her body warm against his. He pulled her closer, and she pressed her lips against his, her fingers dancing through his hair as she deepened their kiss. Lochlan growled as her fingertips traced the shape of his pointed ears. A shiver shot through him at the simple touch.

"Do me." She broke away, turning her back to him with a nervous laugh.

"What?" His kiss addled brain couldn't grasp what she was saying.

"Rinse the mud off my back."

"I can do that." He murmured in her ear, scooping up a handful of water he let his hands slide down her back until the tension left her shoulders and the last of the mud rinsed away.

"Thank you, Brea."

"For what?" She murmured in a sleepy voice.

"For keeping my mind off things I can't fix right now." He pressed a kiss against her throat and took her hand to lead her back to camp.

Traveling over the mountain pass, through the Northern Vatlands and into Iskalt took longer than expected after a fresh snowfall left them seeking a different path—and warm clothes for Brea. She hadn't thought that far ahead when she packed her things to follow.

It felt good to be home—doubly so having Brea with him. Part of him wanted to show her his home, but he wasn't here for sightseeing. He had a village to inspect.

"Are we there yet?" Brea asked.

"Almost. The village lies in the valley below. You can just make out the buildings on main street."

"Oh, I see it." Brea leaned over her saddle. "It's bigger than I thought."

"It's a milling town. They have a thriving economy and are remarkably self sustaining this far from the capital city.

"It's like a little Alpine village." Brea smiled. "It's adorable."

"There's a nice inn where we'll stay tonight. The men can make camp just outside the village while we investigate these strange deaths."

"I'm looking forward to a warm bed and a hot meal."

"We used to come here often when I was a kid. I still remember the candy shop and the bakery." Lochlan realized he was more eager to show Brea around the village than finding out what his uncle was up to. He needed to get his head on straight before he let himself get too caught up in Brea and her infectious smiles.

"It's awfully quiet," Brea murmured as they entered the outskirts of town.

Something wasn't right. The village always thrived with activity.

"Loch." Finn slipped off his horse, waving several of Loch's men to fan out behind them with their weapons drawn. Lochlan gave his friend a nod, he could feel it too. Something was very wrong.

"Oh," Brea whispered a moment later as they made their way past the mill. It had snowed recently, but just a light dusting to cover the bodies that lay strewn about. They were all dead.

Dread filled Lochlan's mind as he walked ahead to find villagers laying on the sidewalk and in front of store windows. All dead.

"What happened?" Brea's voice broke with the anguish Lochlan felt at the sight of so much death.

Lochlan stopped at the center of the town square. Children had played here while their parents went about their business in town. He fell to his knees beside a child no more than six, his cold frozen body seemingly unharmed. The boy's lips were blue, and his cold dead eyes stared back at Lochlan with an accusing glare. He should have been here for his people. He should have challenged his uncle for the throne years ago. He was a man now. No longer a boy hiding behind Faolan's skirts. But he'd stood by and let this happen.

"This was powerful magic," Finn whispered. "Callum lost control of it. He's not powerful enough to complete the boundary spell on his own."

"They're burned. Just like the others." Brea bent to examine a little girl with winter flowers in her hair. She didn't deserve this. None of them deserved to have their lives cut short because his uncle was a madman.

Lochlan couldn't breathe. Everywhere he looked he saw dead children. Mothers with their daughters, come to town to sell their ribbons and eggs. Father's stocking up on supplies for the coming winter storm. Shopkeepers and townsfolk just going about their day, all struck down by some kind of insane magical boundary spell his uncle couldn't hope to pull off. Yet he'd sacrificed an entire village just to see if he could do it.

"Finn, send a messenger back to the troops. Tell them to come down from the pass. We have work to do." Brea turned toward the hardware store. "You three." She pointed to the soldiers who'd accompanied them into the village. "Round up all the supplies we'll need."

"For what, my Lady?" the soldier asked.

"These people deserve a final resting place, and we're going to give it to them. We'll need shovels and carts and lots of manpower."

"The ground is frozen, my Lady. In Iskalt they burn their dead and scatter the ashes in the mountain pass."

"Then we'll need to visit the mill for wood for a few pyres. We will not leave these poor people to rot in the sun when the weather warms."

"Yes, my Lady." The soldiers went to do her bidding.

"We'll start with the children." Brea grabbed another group of soldiers and set them to work gathering up the children from the town square and laying them carefully on a wagon bed.

As she issued orders, Lochlan sat in the snow, his heart shattering into a thousand pieces over the unnecessary deaths of his people. People he should have protected.

Before long, Brea had soldiers clearing each building, one by one. She was a natural leader. She led by inspiring others to join her. She never asked them to do anything she wasn't willing to do herself. His men leapt to do her bidding, and Lochlan only hoped that one day he could inspire such loyalty in his people. But he had to protect them first.

"Loch, you're shivering." Brea crouched down at his side. Smoke from the pyres curled into the air, remnants of the people who once gave this village life. They burned the bodies hours ago, but now, as the sun disappeared behind ice-covered trees, Lochlan remained.

"Go away, Brea." He sat on the snowy ground with his knees bent and shoulders hunched forward, watching the smoke drift through the dusk to cover the village in a thick cloud.

Had it really only been the day before she sat next to Lochlan in a mud bath and felt his lips on hers?

That moment and this one didn't belong in the same world.

Lowering herself to the snow beside him, Brea focused on the breath releasing from her mouth in long streams of steam. She was no stranger to harsh winters, having grown up in Ohio, but this was different, more pronounced. She couldn't remember ever feeling so cold, like ice invaded her veins.

But that had little to do with the temperatures, so different from the heat of Eldur. The first leg of their journey into the Northern Vatlands, the temperatures grew progressively colder, but once they crossed the border into Iskalt, the sudden shift to epic freezing took Brea by surprise.

She'd never understand the fae world, or the magic it possessed.

Lochlan hung his head as darkness invaded the sky, and still, they remained silently side by side. He didn't need a pep talk, or for someone to tell him to rise and return to the men camped outside the now empty village.

Wrapping her cloak tighter around herself, she leaned on her knees. Snow seeped into her riding pants, but she was past caring.

"I was four when I left Iskalt." Lochlan's voice carried with it all the pain of this day. "Four when my parents died, when this kingdom became nothing more than a dream to me, a some-day possibility. I always told myself I'd reclaim it one day, but while I had one-days and maybes and a warm palace in Eldur to keep me safe, real people have suffered."

"It's not your fault," Brea whispered.

"Isn't it?" He turned tortured eyes on her, shining with power as the moon rose overhead. "I should be their king, Brea. You wouldn't understand what that means."

"I know it means you feel guilty."

"Guilty? That doesn't begin to describe what I'm feeling. You are heir to the Eldurian throne, yet you do not want it. Nothing stands in your way of taking that crown once your mother relinquishes it. I am a prince with little hope of ever wearing the crown I've dreamed of my entire life."

"It's not fair. You should get to rule a kingdom, not me."

He lifted his eyes to the smoke once more. "Fair does not matter in this world. I want to do what is right. And I've failed. I was too late to save them."

"So, what are you going to do about it?"

He met her gaze. "It is done, Brea. There is nothing I can do."

"I call bullcrap."

"What?"

"You heard me. Sure, you can't save this village, but how many are there in Iskalt?"

"One hundred and eleven—now ten."

"Wow, I did not expect you to know that." She pushed herself to her feet and looked down at him. "Then we have work to do."

"I do not understand."

She sighed. "You fae need everything spelled out, don't you?"

"You're—"

"One of you, I know. You're like a broken record, Loch—and no I won't explain that because we have more important things to do."

"I already told you, this village is lost to us."

"And it's all your fault. Yes, I've heard. But there are a hundred and eight—"

"Ten."

She waved his correction off. "—Villages in this freeze-your-butt-off kingdom. I might not be the most reliable person to say this, being that I'm an heir to two kingdoms and want to go hide in a cave, but maybe it's time."

"Time for what?"

"For you to do what I know you're dying to do. Take back your kingdom."

His mouth opened, but no words came out.

She continued. "I know. You kind of want to kiss me again right now, don't you?"

He cleared his throat. "Brea, now isn't the time, but I need you to know, that was a moment of desperation. I've been terrified since the moment the messenger arrived in Eldur telling us what was happening in Iskalt. You were just kind of—"

"There? Yeah, I get it. Two fae royals get into a mud bath. There has to be a joke in there somewhere. But Loch, this isn't about us right now. I know you're hurting. I know what it feels like to let people down. But just because something shakes your faith and makes you feel like the worst human being on the planet doesn't mean it's time to stop fighting. Maybe it's a signal to start."

Lochlan rose to stand in front of her, the moonlight shining off his pale hair streaked with soot. "I'm not a human being, Brea." He turned on his heel and marched away, the snow crunching underneath his boots.

Brea stayed frozen in place, wondering how she'd failed so spectacularly in her pep talk.

Lochlan didn't need her. It didn't matter how good his lips felt against hers or how much she wanted to kiss him again, she wasn't the person who should be at his side.

"Alona should be here," she whispered. Brea didn't know the human girl she'd been exchanged with, but what she did know was that this life belonged to her. Faolan, Tierney, the crown, Lochlan... Brea was living Alona's life and doing it poorly.

She trudged back to camp where soldiers sat around fledgling fires barely speaking. The day had been filled with horrors, and the Eldurian warriors had to use their magic to light pyres for dead women and children.

None of them would forget what happened here.

Soldiers nodded to Brea as she passed. If they wondered why the Fargelsian princess had come, they didn't voice the thought. One day, when she was revealed to be Eldurian, they'd know she belonged among them.

Lochlan was nowhere in sight, but Finn sat near the far edge of camp on his own in front of sputtering flames. Once night had fallen, the Eldurians could no longer use their magic to keep their fires alive.

Finn looked up as she approached, but the usual smile didn't tilt his lips. "Dóiteán."

"What?" She sat beside him on the blanket he perched on and leaned into him for warmth.

"It's the Fargelsian word for fire. I know no one has

taught you how to use that side of your magic, but they use words to control it."

"Like spells."

He shrugged. "I figured your Fargelsi power would be easy to control without the Eldurian magic tainting it at night. Worth a shot because I'm freezing my bum off here."

Brea pursed her lips and studied the tiny flame that looked like it would die with one more big gust of wind. He was right. She might as well try. If she burned down the camp, at least they'd all be able to warm themselves near the fire.

Reaching one hand out, she let the weaker Fargelsian power pool in her fingertips. It didn't carry the explosiveness of her Eldurian magic. "Dóiteán," she whispered.

Nothing happened.

"Dóiteán," she said, louder this time.

A pop cracked through the air before flames spread over the sticks. Brea and Finn scooted back to avoid being burned, but a triumphant feeling surged through Brea.

She'd done it.

Lochlan ran out of a nearby tent as the other soldiers searched for the source of the sound. When they found Finn and Brea's fire, they rushed over, crowding around the warmth.

"I'll be right back." Brea went to each of the other fires, repeating that single word. By the time she'd finished, weariness overcame her. She stumbled back to where Lochlan stood across the fire from Finn.

"You shouldn't be using your magic." He crossed his arms. "You can't control it."

"I believe I just did." She didn't appreciate the harshness of his tone—even if he was hurting. "You could have made those fires, and you didn't. So, somebody had to."

He pointed to Finn. "You shouldn't encourage her."

"You're right." Finn ducked his head. "I'm sorry."

Lochlan grunted and retreated to his tent.

"You can't honestly believe he was right." Brea fell to her knees and held her hands toward the flames.

Finn sighed. "He does not need me to argue with him right now."

She settled in beside him once more. "Loch thinks this was his fault."

He rubbed his face but didn't respond.

"I think..." Brea sucked in a breath. "I know this is a totally illogical thought, but I can't help thinking part of the blame for the state of Iskalt rests with me."

Finn snorted. "Brea—"

"No, hear me out. I think... Lochlan's parents died saving me from my aunt. They left their kingdom to bring me to the human realm, and somehow, Regan had them killed before they returned. Lochlan and Griff lost their parents, but Iskalt lost its royals. Because of me, Iskalt is now under the rule of a cruel man. And for what? So I can be some sort of weapon against my aunt? That's why I was born, right? But I can barely control this magic." Her voice lowered. "All this death, the horrors from this village that I will never forget, what if it was all for nothing?"

"You are not nothing, Brea. Some would say you're everything."

She remembered Griff telling her that same thing, but it had been another one of his devious lies.

"What would Alona do?" She bumped his shoulder. "If she were here, what would she say to Loch?"

"Alona had a much quieter strength than you." A sad smile curved his lips.

"Are you saying I'm loud? Or pushy?"

He shook his head. "Alona and Lochlan had a friendship few could interpret. Sometimes it was like they spoke their own language, that of siblings."

"Myles and I had that." She smiled at the memory. They could communicate what they were feeling with a single touch or nod.

"Lochlan will always do what is right, Brea. He doesn't need someone to tell him he must fight for his people or what his next move should be. He's not an Eldurian villager that must be convinced to join the next campaign. Alona would have known that. Lochlan would tell her to leave him alone, but she'd join him anyway."

"And then what?"

"She'd just be there. No speeches. No arguing." He smirked at her.

"I don't argue."

He only stared at her. "Lochlan is fully capable of shouldering his own pain and that of everyone else. He's a stubborn brute like that. But Alona wouldn't have let him, because pain like his—a life-long struggle with duty and power—it's enough to harden even the most joyful fae. And Alona refused to let Loch become a man of stone."

"It sounds like she's a good friend."

Finn looked away. "He needs you, Brea. He will never admit it, but I've known from the moment I met you why."

"Are you going to enlighten me?"

"No." He leaned back, stretching out beside the fire and closing his eyes. "I don't think I will."

Brea didn't know how long she stared into the flickering flames, her damp cloak finally drying as she scooted closer to the warmth.

Finn's words ran on a constant loop through her mind. He was wrong. Lochlan needed Alona, his best friend, not her. He needed Alona like she needed Myles. Completely and without reservation.

Yet, as they camped beside a village of the dead, Alona and Myles were prisoners of the queen who made this possible. Callum O'Shea tried using Regan's spell to create a barrier, but Iskalt magic didn't work like Fargelsian. There were bound to be repercussions.

Brea knew hardly anything about the power, and even she knew that.

What was Callum playing at?

Had he wanted Lochlan to see this? Maybe it was a test... or a signal of more to come.

Brea sat up straighter as a thought came to her. He

couldn't have believed it would work. Iskalt was trying to draw Eldur into a war.

It was the only thing that made sense. If he performed enough atrocities on his people, Callum knew Lochlan would have to respond—probably with the might of the Eldurian army.

But there was one thing Callum didn't know. Queen Faolan had grown into an isolationist, not wanting to send her people to fight another's war.

Brea jumped to her feet and paced in front of the fire. She had to tell someone, but why would they listen to a girl who knew nothing of war? Back in the human world, the closest she got to battle was watching some of the men in her town join the military.

Glancing toward Lochlan's tent nearby, she knew he'd at least hear her out. Her long strides took her to the tent, and she considered knocking, but the fae cared nothing for privacy, and she was half-convinced he wouldn't let her in.

Pushing the tent flap aside, her eyes widened when a wave of warm air hit her. The tent was... heated?

Lochlan sat on the edge of his bed roll, his legs stretched out in front of him and his head in his hands. He didn't move as she entered.

A light glowed from somewhere in the tent, but she couldn't figure out the source. Its glow reflected off Lochlan's bare chest. The man loved to be half naked—a fact Brea was not the least bit upset about.

"Loch." Her voice was small, tentative. "How is it warm in here?"

He didn't lift his head. "I am of Iskalt, Lady Brea."

"Right." His magic worked at night. She didn't appreciate his sudden formality, but this moment wasn't about her.

All thoughts of telling him about her suspicions flew from her mind as she stared down at him. Instead, she thought of what Finn had said. Brea would give anything to feel like Myles was with her. Maybe Lochlan felt the same about Alona.

Holding her usual word-vomit in, Brea channeled the quiet princess she'd heard so much about. Lowering herself to her knees at his side, she leaned forward and wrapped her arms around him in an awkward hug.

His body stiffened, and he tried to pull away.

Brea held on tighter. "I'm here," she whispered. "You don't have to say anything. Today was horrible, and I get the feeling the days coming will only get worse. It's okay to let yourself feel the pain, Loch." She rested her chin on the heated skin of his shoulder.

His stubble scratched against her, but she didn't move. Tonight wasn't about the kiss they'd shared or the anger that seemed to always stand between them. This moment was an acknowledgement of two facts: nothing coming would be easy, and they were in this together as friends and allies.

His body relaxed into hers, and he buried his face in her hair. They stayed in their embrace, both taking comfort in not being alone.

The images from that day would never leave their minds, but the false Iskalt king would pay.

Just as Regan would pay for taking Alona and Myles.

"Brea," Lochlan whispered, lifting his head.

She leaned back and met his gaze.

"It wasn't all for nothing."

She sucked in a breath. He'd heard what she'd said to Finn about Loch's parents. "I—"

He pulled her back into their hug. "No. Don't refute it. You're the key. I've known it since the very first time I saw you in the human realm."

"I may be a key, but what door do I unlock?" The one that gets her friends kidnapped by an evil queen, or the one leading to an incompetent practically-human girl sitting on the throne of Eldur?

"I guess we'll see."

Yes, they would. She wouldn't have believed this a few months ago, but she and Lochlan might be on the same side. It wasn't the side of Fargelsi or the Eldurian crown. Not the side of Iskalt or this magic they both possessed.

They would do what was right for the people they cared about—whether that was Alona and Myles or nameless villagers in a distant kingdom.

As Brea sat beside Lochlan and let him feel his pain, she no longer had to channel Alona, because she wasn't her, and she'd made herself believe the people in this new life of hers needed Brea Robinson just as much.

Traveling back through the mountain pass into the Northern Vatlands, Lochlan set an urgent pace. If he was eager to reach Iskalt on the trip coming, returning, he was like a man possessed, never letting them make camp for more than a few hours before they moved on.

Brea just hoped her mother would have the heart and the sense to help Lochlan protect his people. It didn't matter if it led to a war Faolan didn't want. With the death of an entire Iskalt village, this was about common decency and respect for all life—not just Eldurian life.

"Will you help me convince the queen that Callum needs to be stopped?" Lochlan rode beside her along the Southern road that would lead them into Raudur City in less than an hour.

"I don't know how much help I'll be, but I will try."

"She listens to you, Brea. You're the reason I had help on this trip. She wasn't going to allow it until you spoke your mind."

"Hopefully, my mother will see the sense in coming to Iskalt's aid before it's too late." Brea urged her horse to keep up with Lochlan's. She could just make out the tiered gardens in the fading sunlight. She was eager for a nice hot bath and her own bed, but she imagined they all had a long night ahead of them first.

Lochlan leaped off his horse the moment they passed through the palace gates into the courtyard. "Meet me in the throne room in ten minutes."

"Which one of us was he talking to?" Brea glanced at Finn, looking exhausted after their mad dash across the Eldur desert.

"Unfortunately, I think he means both of us." Finn tossed his reins to a servant and followed Lochlan into the palace.

Brea slipped off Sassa's back, patting her long white mane. "Thanks for the ride, girl. Master Arturo will be happy to have you back." She handed the reins off to another servant, heading inside the cool interior of the palace, stopping only long enough to splash water on her face at the fountain and take a long gulp of the refreshing basil and berry infused water the servants made ready for visitors to the palace.

"Brea, darling, we were so worried." Tierney crept up behind her on her way to the throne room.

"I'm sorry, Mom, I just couldn't let him do this alone."

Brea wiped a hand over her tired eyes. "I didn't mean to worry you."

Tierney stifled a gasp, taking Brea's hand as she fell in step beside her.

"What?" Brea asked.

"It's nothing, dear." Tierney patted her hand. "That was just the first time you've called me Mom without forcing it."

"Oh, well, that's not nothing then, is it?" Brea smiled at the sweetest of her mothers. It was so easy to love Tierney. Faolan was harder, but Brea suspected that was because they were both so stubborn.

"I fear this report will be worse than the last." Tierney led Brea into the throne room where Lochlan and Faolan were already at odds with each other. "Oh, dear." She gasped at the look on Lochlan's face. "Our poor boy has had a shock, hasn't he?"

Brea gripped her mother's hand. "You've no idea."

"Please, your Majesty," Lochlan said. "If you could have seen it with your own eyes. Helpless children lying dead in the town square, covered in snow. Men and women going about their business one moment and dead the next—the whole village sacrificed for a magical experiment that had no hope of succeeding. It can't be ignored."

"I understand your anger and frustration, Lochlan, I do. But this is not a matter for Eldur. If you took a step back from the horror of it all, you would see that is exactly what your uncle wants."

"That's what I thought too." Brea stepped forward. "Callum O'Shea knew his experiment wouldn't work, but he slaughtered all those people anyway. He wants to lure you into a conflict."

Lochlan's face paled at her remarks, like he thought she'd just betrayed him by agreeing with her mother.

Faolan gave her daughter a nod of approval. "We cannot allow such a distraction at this time. We must keep our focus on Regan. Our troops at the Fargelsian border are working to bring the barrier down, and then we are going to bring my daughter home. And I will speak to you later about your disobedience, running off to join the troops like a common woman. It is not for a princess of Eldur to get involved with the dealings of Iskalt."

"But I am not a princess of Eldur, am I, mother? You've made me a princess of Fargelsi, escaped from the realm to come to Eldur's aid. But according to your politics, why would I get involved in Eldur's issues with Gelsi if you can't be bothered to help with Iskalt?"

"Do not twist my words, child."

"You forget I come from the human world where we help those in need no matter where their loyalties lie. When a disaster happens, it doesn't matter if they're American, Chinese, or British. Rich or poor. They're all people, and when it comes to the loss of life, politics don't matter. And I'm eighteen. In *my* world that means I don't need your permission to make my own decisions."

"What would you have me do? Divide my army and invade Iskalt and Gelsi at the same time? Abandon my efforts to bring Alona home? Or your friend, Myles? Regan and Callum want to divide us, and so far it's working."

Faolan stepped down from her throne, taking Lochlan's hands in hers.

"I know how much this hurts. How you feel torn in two, but one day you will rule Isklat, of that I have no doubt." The queen reached for Brea's hand. "And one day you will rule Eldur. That bright future is the one I fight for every day. You will be the greatest of allies, but we must be strong and stay focused on the direct threat, which is Regan."

"He will strike again," Lochlan said. "And next time it will be closer to home. Callum O'Shea will draw you into this conflict. How many lives must be lost for you to see that? Will it take Eldurian spilled blood?"

"That's not fair, Lochlan. I care for your people, I do, but my priority will always be Eldur first. Once we deal with Regan's direct threat to Eldur and bring Alona and Myles home, Callum will back down. Let's cut off the head of the dragon and the rest will fall into place."

"I cannot wait while more innocent people are slaughtered. I must return to Iskalt." Lochlan stood with his head held high. "It is time I put my people first the way you have always put Eldur first. I will leave tomorrow."

"Please stay a few days before you leave us again," Tierney interjected. "We understand your need to be with your people, Lochlan. You are their rightful ruler, and it was only a matter of time before you were ready to challenge your uncle. We support that." Tierney met her wife's dark gaze with one of her own. A battle of wills happened in that single instant, but whatever it was, Tierney won.

"We do support you, Lochlan. But we are sad to see you

go. Please, give your troop of volunteers a few days to rest. If they are still willing, they may accompany you into Iskalt. I won't have you leaving entirely on your own."

Brea watched the subtle way her parents communicated, and she realized Tierney was the Faolan whisperer. She needed to take lessons from her mom to learn how to communicate with her formidable mother.

"I will go with Lochlan," Brea announced. "Just long enough to help you gather your countrymen and those who would support your claim for the Iskalt throne. You're not very good with the talking. I'd like to help you, if you'll have me."

"You should stay here where it's safe," Lochlan muttered.

"That wasn't a no, so I'll take it as a yes." Brea turned to her parents. "Mothers, I will be careful and will return in a few weeks. I'd just like the opportunity to do what I can to help Lochlan. I could use the time away to wrap my mind around the idea that one day I may rule Eldur. At the moment, that is simply not something I can even consider for my future."

"I cannot allow you to leave, Brea," Faolan insisted.

"Good thing I'm not asking." Brea turned to leave without the queen's dismissal. It didn't matter what her mother wanted, Brea refused to let Lochlan walk out that door not knowing he had the assistance he needed to take his throne. If her mother couldn't give him that, then the only thing Brea knew to do was go with him to help in whatever ways she could.

"I thought I might find you here."

Brea looked up from her spot on the grass to find Finn sitting on the paddock fence, watching her with the young ponies.

"I tried to get back to work today, but Master Arturo said there was no point if I'm just leaving again in a few days. Apparently, the man knows everything."

"He'll outfit Loch's unit with fresh mounts. The stables master always knows what's going on before the rest of us do." Finn came to sit with her while the young foals tested out their gangly legs in a wobbly game of tag. "What are their names?"

"Dawn and Dusk." Brea smiled at their innocence. "I thought when they're full grown, Dusk could be mine, and Dawn could be Alona's."

"She would love that." Finn's voice sounded far away. About as far away as the Gelsi dungeons.

"You're as torn as I am, aren't you?" Brea picked a wildflower and wrapped the stem around her finger like a ring. For a moment it reminded her of that time with Griff when she'd almost picked a poisonous flower. Everything in Gelsi was poisonous, but she never had to worry about that in Eldur. Here, nature was always exactly what it seemed. The people, sometimes less so.

"I feel trapped. Like I can't possibly split myself in half to help the two most important people in my life when they need it most. The moment I heard the queen sent her army to the Fargelsi border, I wanted to go. I need to do my part. I need to be there when Alona is freed. But Loch needs me too. I can't abandon him now."

"Loch will understand, Finn. Alona needs you. Let me be your other half. I'll be with Loch."

"You're right." Finn rubbed a tired hand over his eyes. "The queen is sending fresh troops to the border in two days. I will leave with them after I talk to Loch."

"Milord?"

Brea and Finn turned toward the weak voice. They saw her just as she collapsed.

"Who is she?" Brea asked as they raced toward the young girl.

"By the looks of her she's from Eldfal."

"Isn't that north of Loch Sol?" Brea was proud of her growing knowledge of fae geography.

"Yes."

"Did this kid just walk across the desert by herself?"

"Barefoot by the looks of it." Finn examined her blistered feet. "She needs water." Finn grabbed his canteen and propped the girl's head up.

"Need to see the queen, milord," the girl murmured.

"We'll take you to the queen soon. Drink a bit of water for me first, and then we'll go." Finn tipped a trickle of water into her mouth, coaxing her to drink slowly.

"How could she survive such a journey? She can't be more than ten." Brea checked her pulse. It was strong but much too fast.

"Sheer willpower." Finn picked her up. "Let's get her to the healers."

"I need to see the queen," the girl insisted. "I have an important message for her."

"How about you tell me your message, and I'll deliver it to the queen myself while you get some rest?"

"No. None but the queen herself should hear this news."

"She has every right to bring her grievances and concerns to the queen like everyone else who comes to the palace." Brea examined the girl's feet as they made their way back down to the palace. It was a miracle she was still walking when she found them in the paddock.

"Then let's get some more water into her so she can speak to her queen."

They paused every few minutes so the girl could take slow sips of water.

"What's your name, sweetheart?" Brea asked.

"Bailee." With each sip, she seemed to grow stronger. "I think I can walk now."

"Not on those poor feet, you can't." Finn refused to set her down.

"Are you sure you won't let us take you to the palace healers first? Some mud from Loch Sol would give you instant relief for your feet."

Bailie's eyes misted with tears. "No, milady, I must see the queen. Even if I have to wait in line all day."

"Well, you're in luck. We have a move-to-the-front-of-the-line card with your name on it. And when you're done giving your message to the queen, you can have all the pastries you want from the table in the throne room.

"And then you're going straight to the healer's, young lady."

"Oh, I'm no lady, milord. Just a village girl from Eldfal." Her lower lip trembled, and her face filled with a soul-crushing grief. This poor girl had been through something awful.

As they entered the palace courtyard, Brea jogged ahead to retrieve a bundle of cooling towels and berry-infused water for Bailee.

"Drink this," she ordered while mopping the girl's dirty face with a cool towel.

"Oh thank you, milady. That feels nice."

Brea wrapped the other cloths around Bailee's feet.

Making their way into the throne room, Brea groaned at the line of villagers come to seek audience with their queen. She hated to steamroll over them, but Bailee needed rest.

"Your Majesty." Finn approached the throne. "Pardon the interruption, but Princess Brea and I found this child up near the North Road. She's come from Eldfal with a message for your ears alone.

"She walked all that way on her own?" Faolan stepped from her throne to greet the girl. "She should go straight to the healers this instant."

"She won't hear of it, your Majesty," Brea said, hoping for once her mother would act like a genuine person with a conscious rather than the queen.

"Set her down, Finn." Faolan guided them to a chair meant for the nobles.

"Her name is Bailee," Brea whispered.

"Bailee." Faolan crouched down so she was on a level with the girl. "What message have you brought for me from Eldfal?"

"Oh, Majesty, it was awful." Bailee's eyes filled with tears. "It was Mount Eldfal, madame. It erupted four nights ago. I came as quickly as I could."

"And you were such a brave girl to do that all on your own. Mount Eldfal hasn't erupted in centuries. We've had no reports of any sign that it might no longer be dormant."

"It was the soldiers, Majesty," Bailee said. "They came, just a few of them. They did it at night so we couldn't protect ourselves with our magic, ma'am. We've all been taught since we was young how to shield ourselves against the mountain if it should erupt. I've never seen it happen in all mi life, ma'am. I was with the flock when it happened. I have a pregnant ewe about to give birth, so I've been staying the night out on the plains in case she needs help in the night."

"These soldiers, where did they come from, Bailee?" The queen asked. "Did you recognize them?"

Bailee nodded. "They came from across the sea. I seen their ship when they came from Iskalt. They headed straight for the mountain at dusk, ma'am. They made the mountain rumble with their magic."

"What happened when Eldfal erupted?"

"It happened so fast, mi Majesty." Bailee dropped her head, great big tears splashing on her hand. "The lava moved quick as a flash, ma'am. It destroyed everything and everyone in its path."

"What of the village?"

"There's nothing left, mi Majesty," Bailee said in a choked whisper. "Nothing at all. Just me."

"Oh, my darling girl." Queen Faolan swept the girl up into her arms ran a comforting hand over her hair. "You are so very brave and smart to come straight here. Don't you worry about it anymore. I will take care of it from here. I want you to go with my good friend, Finn and see the healers and get some rest. I will come visit you soon."

"Yes. Thank you." Bailee tried to stand, but Finn picked her up and headed for the exit.

"Loch was right," Brea said, turning her attention on her mother. "This is Callum's doing. He's destroyed an Eldurian village."

"Is it true?" Lochlan stormed into the throne room, scattering the citizens waiting in line to speak with the queen. "Eldfal is no more?"

"We don't yet know the extent of it," Faolan said, returning to her throne. "At this time, I will ask our citizens to please return tomorrow. We must clear the throne room immediately so we may discuss this threat on Eldur and decide our next moves."

Lochlan waited impatiently for the commoners to leave. As he paced like a caged lion, Brea knew he was at his breaking point.

The moment the double doors closed, Lochlan turned on the queen. "I told you it would come to this, but even I didn't realize it would happen so soon. Callum must be stopped, your Majesty."

"I did not think he would have the gall to make such a blatant move against me." Faolan sat back against her throne, unable to meet Lochlan's beseeching gaze. "I stand by my decisions, Lochlan. I believe Callum and Regan mean to distract me and divide my forces, knowing I cannot sit by while Eldur burns."

"Then *do* something," Brea begged.

"I will not recall my army from the border. Regan still poses the greatest threat against us—and by us, I mean Eldur and our Iskalt brothers and sisters."

"We must do something for Iskalt and for all those Eldurians who died." Brea shared a desperate look with Lochlan.

"And we shall." Faolan stood from her throne, crossing the room to a desk against the wall. "I will call in our militia on a voluntary basis. Give me two days to gather what forces I can, and you may lead them against Callum along with your seasoned unit of three hundred volunteers. That is the best I can do."

"It will have to be enough." Lochlan nodded. "I will gather Iskalt soldiers and militia along the way."

"Where will you attack?" Brea asked.

"This is not a mission that will lead to battle right away," Lochlan said. "This is a campaign to gain the support of my people and grow my army before I seize the throne from my uncle once and for all."

The militias weren't coming. Well, some of them were, but not the force that could have made up the greatest part of Lochlan's army, not the Raudur city militia.

Warriors from outlying villages trickled into the capital, and more would come as Lochlan led his force toward Iskalt.

But the people right here in the largest city in Eldur? They sat in their homes, closing their doors against the thought of helping a foreign kingdom.

Brea walked the streets at dusk against her mother's wishes. Sure, there were dangers in any city, but as the sun disappeared, Brea was one of the few in Eldur with magic still coursing through her veins.

Magic she couldn't control without the words she didn't know, but that didn't matter. The people of Eldur still thought her the Fargelsian princess. They didn't know how inexperienced she really was.

As she stared up at the squat buildings, stretching as far as she could see, she couldn't help thinking about another city in another place. Back in the human world, Myles' dad occasionally let her and Myles tag along when he went to Columbus for supplies. It was a two-hour drive north into the city. There were few similarities between those tall towers that reached toward the sky with glass windows reflecting sunlight back into the atmosphere and these heavily adorned sandstone buildings. In place of paved roads, there were cobblestone cart paths.

But the people, they weren't so different. They went about their days working and shopping at the market. Taverns lined the road, not unlike the bars of human cities—serving as a place for people to unwind and let their rowdy out, as Myles would say.

There were mothers and fathers, children chasing each other in games of tag. The poor relied on the charity of strangers, and the wealthy lived in grand homes among the upper city, close to the top of the canyon.

Lord knows, Lochlan would never admit it, but the fae weren't so different from humans. They desired love and comfort.

Brea stopped outside Xander's tavern in the lower city market. At this time of day, the fae inside would be drinking mead instead of Eldur brew. The door opened and a young couple stumbled out, almost falling down in laughter as they headed up the road.

Loud chatter filtered out of the tavern, and Brea propped the door open with her foot, peering in. She was an outsider getting a glimpse at a simple fae life. Most of the time, she still thought of herself as human, different from the fae around her. But staring into the crowded room, Brea wanted to be one of them, just once. She wanted to know what it was to belong, not simply because she was supposedly a princess and future queen, but because these fae seemed to take such pleasure in just being together.

Her eyes followed Adamina as she wound around tables, two mugs of mead in hand. She set them on a table in the back corner where two familiar fae took them gratefully.

Brea entered the tavern, letting the door swing shut behind her. Her dress caught between her legs, and she stepped forward, wishing she'd worn something different into the city. The leather bodice suddenly felt too constricting, cutting off her breath. The room started spinning and didn't stop until a hand landed on her shoulder.

"Princess." Xander's gruff voice calmed her. She hated the title he used, but at least he didn't try to bow. "Are you okay?"

She nodded. "I'm good, Xander. Thank you. The last few days have been trying, and I'm just a little tired." She'd been working herself to the bone getting all the arriving militias accounted for and equipped. She'd convinced Lochlan to stay longer than he'd planned, but as the day of their departure neared, the doubts entered her mind.

How could she expect to be any help to him?

What if they failed?

Shouldn't she go with Finn to Fargelsi?

But what would Myles do? What was right? He'd tell her there was nothing she could do for him. If there was a way to free him, she'd go to any length, but there wasn't. So, Iskalt it was.

She forced a smile and looked to Xander. "Yes. I wish to speak with Lochlan."

"Would you like some mead?"

Her face screwed up in disgust. "Um, no. An Eldur Brew will be fine."

One side of his mouth curved up. "I'll have Mina bring it to you."

This time, her smile was genuine. "Thank you."

Tables quieted as she passed, and she wasn't sure she'd ever get used to that. What would happen when they learned she was the Eldurian heir?

Lochlan and Finn didn't see her until she practically collapsed into the booth across from them. They looked up from where they'd been huddled in conversation on the same side of table. Brea could see it as she looked at them, how they were once drawn to each other when they were younger.

Lochlan with his light looks and dark countenance. Finn with his sparkling eyes and the way he could find joy even when his heart had been ripped from his body.

"Shouldn't you be up at the palace?" Lochlan lifted a brow, but there was no scolding in his voice.

He'd seemed to have forgotten all about their kiss, but

that was fine with Brea when he said things that infuriated her so much. "Shouldn't you?" she challenged.

Finn chortled as he sipped his mead.

Brea held Loch's gaze until Adamina set a mug of Eldur Brew in front of her. "Thank you, Mina. I know you probably had to make this special at this time of day."

Adamina smiled down at her. "Anything for you, Brea. Let me know when you need another." She shot a look at Lochlan. "Something tells me you might need it with this kind of company."

Brea hid her smile behind her mug as Adamina flounced away.

"I don't think Mina likes you, Loch." Finn shoved his shoulder with a laugh.

"That's because few in this city like the foreign prince who thinks he's better than them." Brea shrugged.

It wasn't a lie. She'd spent a lot of time among these people, and they held no loyalty for Lochlan. In their opinion, he was a pushy brute. They weren't wrong.

"I don't need people to love me." Lochlan drained his mug and held it in the air, a silent call to Adamina for more. He waved it impatiently.

As Adamina set another in front of him and took the empty mug, she muttered something like "fool of a man."

Brea shook her head. "It's a wonder they don't like you. You're very courteous."

"Was that supposed to be human sarcasm?" Lochlan scowled. "It does not become you."

"Then it's a good thing your opinion is of little import—as you'd say in your haughty way."

"Children." Finn leaned forward with his elbows on the table. "You were playing so nice on our jaunt into Iskalt."

"Jaunt." Lochlan snorted with a shake of his head.

He was right. There was nothing jaunt-like about the trip. Only death. Fear and grief overcame the loathing for a few short days, but now she was pretty sure Lochlan was back to hating her.

She didn't hate him, that much she'd realized, but she wasn't quite sure how to stop arguing with him when he was such a disagreeable fae. As tensions rose in the palace with the militias preparing to march into Iskalt, the tensions between Lochlan and Brea grew more strained.

"I don't need people to like me," Lochlan grumbled as he sipped his mead. "Their respect is enough."

There was something sad in that statement, and for a moment Brea wanted to reach across the table and put her hand over his. The pain had never left Lochlan's eyes, no matter how hard he tried to cover it up.

She lowered her voice. "Wouldn't you rather they respect you out of love instead of fear?"

"They will never love me, Brea. You need to understand... those in the fae realms are hesitant about outsiders. Eldur is not my kingdom. I may have grown up here, but they are not my people. And for that reason, they will not trust me."

"But they like me." At least she thought they did. "And they think I'm a Fargelsian princess."

"Fargelsi has kidnapped their beloved princess, and you show up having escaped Queen Regan. Don't you see, Brea? You give them hope for Alona."

"Hope," she whispered to herself. It was the most honest thing anyone had ever said to her. She'd spent her life being told she was crazy and that no one other than Myles ever loved her. But now...

Finn spoke as if reading the thought out loud. "I see it too. They barely know you, yet you have their love. If you can escape Gelsi, why can't Alona?"

They all knew the reasons it would be harder for Alona. She was a human with no magic, and Regan was no doubt keeping her in more secure holdings. But Brea saw what Finn and Lochlan meant.

She sipped her Eldur Brew in silence, wondering if this hope they claimed she gave the people actually meant anything at all.

Eldur Brew was the devil.

Brea lay awake in her bed, unable to sleep. She'd returned from the tavern hours ago, leaving Lochlan and Finn to their cups, but it seemed this sleepless night would only add to her weariness.

Her mother convinced Lochlan to wait three more days for more militia to arrive. Most brought their own horses, but the palace armory had been busy arming them with adequate weapons rather than the more rudimentary ones they'd brought.

Everything was moving as it should. Wagons of supplies were loaded and ready to accompany the force. It wouldn't be easy. Most of these fae hadn't seen a battle in their lifetimes, and others not for many years. They weren't the seasoned warriors making up the Eldurian army that now sat on the Fargelsi border.

But they were all Lochlan had.

Brea rolled over, burying her face in her pillow. How did she get here? In three days, she'd ride away from her mother's palace in fighting leathers, armed with a sword she didn't know how to use and magic she had a tenuous control over.

Yep, this probably wouldn't end well for Brea.

But she had no other choice. With Finn leaving for Fargelsi soon, she had to be by Lochlan's side. Despite their arguing and constant insults, if anything happened to him, she... a groan rattled in her throat. It would be so much easier if she could hate him, if he'd shown himself to be the snake his brother was.

Thoughts of Griff sent warring emotions through her. She'd thought he was the first person other than Myles to ever truly see her, but it was all a beautiful lie.

A thud sounded against her door, and she lifted her head, sighing as she kicked the sheets from her legs. If she could be sure she wouldn't destroy the entire palace by doing it, she'd reach out with her magic and pull the door open.

But alas, she had to use her legs.

Yanking the door open, she prepared to unleash her rage

on whoever stood on the other side. Instead, she rolled her eyes. "You've made quite the habit of showing up at my room in the middle of the night." She held her arm across the doorway so Lochlan couldn't enter.

But when he lifted his icy blue eyes to hers, magic swirled in their depths, and it was so beautiful she dropped her arm. "I need your help."

There was no scorn in his voice, only desperation, so Brea gestured for him to enter.

He walked in, his eyes skimming over the discarded clothes strewn over the floor and other possessions out of place. Brea hadn't let Rowena in to tidy up once she'd gotten back from the city. The maid needed sleep too.

"Want some tea?" Brea asked.

"I'm okay."

"Good, because it's cold, anyway." She scooped clothes off the floor and set them on the end of her bed before leading Lochlan to the sitting area. They hadn't been alone together since she comforted him outside the village of the dead, and the silence stretched like a vast sea, seemingly insurmountable.

Crouching in front of the hearth, Brea whispered "Dóiteán" and flames licked up over the logs, casting a glow across the room.

Lochlan sat down and scrubbed a hand through his hair and down over the long tail.

Brea straightened and walked toward him, taking a seat next to him on the couch—settee as those in the palace called it—so close their legs touched. Lochlan didn't move away from her.

She nudged his shoulder. "You said you needed my help."

He nodded. "I don't really know where to start."

"Hey." She took his hand between both of hers. "You can say anything to me. I know your world is bleak right now, but you can do this. You know that, right? You are the rightful king of Iskalt, and the moment you let people see that, see the real you, they won't be able to hold themselves back from supporting you."

He turned to look at her, his eyes holding some emotion she couldn't decipher. "You haven't changed. All these years I've watched you and marveled at your human optimism. No matter what you went through, your strength never wavered. How can you believe there is good in this world when so much bad happens?"

"Because I've seen it. My life has been hell, Loch. There were no palaces or doting parents for me." She paused, not knowing how exactly much he knew of her life, how much he'd seen. But there was no use hiding the darker parts of her, not from him. "The first time they locked me away, I was nine. For three months, I spent all my time with people whose jobs were to figure out what was wrong with me—mentally—why I was having delusions and telling lies. I was institutionalized four more times before my arrest for almost killing Myles."

"I don't see the good in any of that."

"That's because you're not looking. Griff kidnapped me

and trapped me in Fargelsi, but everything I went through, every trial and abuse, it brought me here. Loch, Eldur is the good. You say the people love me, but I love them too. There's a kindness here. I see it every day as more Eldurian fae travel to the palace to join a fight for a kingdom that is not their own."

"I haven't considered any of that."

"Of course, you haven't. You were raised a prince, told that commoners must obey your every command. But they don't have to, not this time. The warriors about to make this journey with us are not here out of obligation. They're here because it's the right thing to do. Only the light can defeat the dark, Lochlan O'Shea."

He flipped his palm over to intertwine their fingers. "Maybe your human traits aren't the burden I thought they were."

"Optimism and faith doesn't have to be just for humans."

"I need you, Brea."

Her breath hitched at the admission.

When he continued, the feeling inside her deflated. "I need the Raudur City militia, but they do not come."

"What can I do about that?"

He released her hand and skimmed his thumb under her chin, tilting it up so she met his gaze. His mouth curved into a half smile. "I need you to make a speech, a call to arms. Say whatever you must. They will come for you in a way they won't for me. You inspire them." He stood, ready to leave once she gave her consent.

"I..." What could she say to his request? She'd never

dreamed of being a princess and didn't want to be a queen. The people of Eldur shouldn't follow her. Who was she but an inadequate fae girl who knew little of their world?

A fae who may as well have been human for all the good she did them.

But there was this man, the one who lost his parents when they saved her life, the very same fae she'd argued with since the day he stole her from the human police station.

For him, she'd do it. For him, she'd do just about anything. Make a speech, go to war, wear the crown.

"How do you know?" she whispered. "That I inspire them?"

His face softened as he realized what her question meant. She'd agreed to help. "Because, Brea..." His voice lowered as he turned away and walked to the door. "Even in my darkest night, you inspire me."

"Where are you going in such a hurry?" Finn jogged to catch up to Lochlan and Brea in the courtyard.

"I have a speech to give." Brea didn't break her stride as she headed toward the lower part of the city where most of the commoners dwelled. Lochlan tried to get her to set out for the queen's market near the palace. It was a lot nicer and more crowded this time of day, but she insisted the people she needed to reach wouldn't be there.

"Wait, you have a what now?"

"A speech. Just call me Greta."

"You're speaking nonsense again, Brea. That's not your name."

"How is that different from most days?" Lochlan said, feeling uncertain about this call to arms. He should do it himself, but he had more faith in Brea's ability to inspire her people to come to his aid.

"Greta Thunberg... she's a human who gives lots of speeches and gets people to act..." Brea paused as if waiting for either of them to react to some joke they didn't understand. "Loch has no personality, but he needs soldiers. Those villagers needed soldiers to protect them in Iskalt and Eldfal. So we're going to get some."

"Where?" Finn fell in step beside her.

"The free market near the docks."

"Do you ... think they sell soldiers at the market?" Finn's smirk would normally make Lochlan laugh, but this was too important. He had too much riding on Brea's ability to win the people of Eldur over to his side.

"Of course not, but that's where the militia will be going about their lives."

"It smells down there." Finn sighed.

"It smells like hard work. We're courting the city's militia today. We have to go where they go. These men and women have jobs that keep them busy. It's likely they don't even know the militia has been called in for volunteers."

"It's not entirely voluntary," Lochlan said. "It's their choice to serve, but the militia is paid handsomely for their service. Many will join for the compensation—if they're moved to fight for the cause."

"Then let's go find a soapbox for me to climb up on."

"The things she says..." Finn shook his head. "You think we'll ever understand her?"

"I doubt it." Lochlan enjoyed the way his best friend and

his—whatever Brea was to him—sparred with words. He couldn't help but think of Alona and the way the four of them would fit together. Someday.

"Neither of you are funny." Brea led them through the upper levels of Raudur city down to the lower regions near the river and the open marketplace where the "normal" people, as she described them, carried out their business.

"Princess Brea," one of the shopkeepers called to her. "I have some new tunics you might like. Nothing as fine as your lovely dresses, but they're perfect for wearing to your apprenticeship with Master Arturo."

"Thank you for thinking of me, Mrs. Milton. I will come by later today. You know how I prefer simple clothes, and I'm in need of some new tunics. My lady's maid has a habit of losing them in the wash."

As they made their way into the heart of the lower city, more people came out to see Brea. Not just to sell her things, but to genuinely connect with her. They followed her without hesitation when she told them why she was here.

"They love her," Finn said, as mesmerized as Lochlan by their response to the unusual princess they still didn't realize was their own.

"See how you make things happen?" Lochlan murmured when they reached the market square to find a crowd waiting for them near the trader's guild.

"Yeah, it takes loads of magic and charisma to ask a bunch of people to come listen to what I have to say when they're already here." Brea shook her head like it was nothing when to him it was everything. That she would do this for him and his people when she had no reason to. Did she not know how rare a person she was?

Brea smiled as she stood at the center of the growing crowd, completely at ease with herself and the relationships she'd built with these people.

"Hi, everyone." She gave a nervous little wave. "I was never good at delivering speeches in school, so I'll just jump right in and say what I came to say. We need your help." She gestured to Lochlan and Finn, not realizing the disdain some of the commoners had for Lochlan and much of the Eldur nobility.

"Little more than a week ago, a village in Iskalt was slaughtered. The usurper king, Callum O'Shea is responsible. He tried to create a magical barrier around an innocent village, replicating the barrier around Fargelsi. His magic failed and killed every man, woman, and child within its borders."

Several gasps echoed through her captive audience. Lochlan couldn't breathe, he was so desperate for this to work. He needed the people to understand what was at stake. That is wasn't just about some foreign village they didn't know or care anything about. It was about them and their families. This was just the beginning of Callum and Regan's potential reign of terror, and it was up to him and Brea to stop it.

"But that's a long way away, right? The problems of another realm. It shouldn't concern us here in Eldur." Several heads nodded in agreement, and Lochlan clenched his fists at his sides. He needed to trust her. Brea had a natural charm and an effortless way of speaking to people. It wasn't his way, but it worked for her.

"But I'm afraid it does. Just a few days ago, several soldiers from Iskalt came into Eldur on King Callum's orders. They visited Eldfal late one night. Using their magic, they caused the mountain to erupt, wiping out the entire village except for one brave girl who traveled across the desert all on her own to warn the queen of this attack. She's just ten years old and a hero. I can't imagine what that poor girl suffered.

"Suffering sucks, doesn't it?" She peered into the crowd. "We all have our burdens to bear. Some suffering is worse than others. But at the end of the day, we're all just fae, right? It doesn't matter if you're from Fargelsi like me, or Eldur, or Iskalt, or even the human realm. We're all people, and when there is needless suffering in the world, it is our responsibility to stand up for those who can't stand up for themselves. It's our job to help them when they just don't have the will or the energy to do it on their own.

"You all know how I escaped from Fargelsi. I couldn't have done it without a very dear friend who helped me—at great risk to her own safety. She didn't have to step up, but if she hadn't, I wouldn't be here. I would still be Queen Regan's pawn.

"Regan O'Rourke is the real enemy. She would like us all slaves to her will—and she'll have it too, if we don't stand up for what is right. Right now, Eldur is surrounded by threats. Regan holds your princess, yet she's in league with Callum, pulling strings to distract our focus so we fail on both fronts.

"But a king stands among us. The rightful king of Iskalt needs your help. With your busy lives, you may not have realized the queen has called in volunteers from the city militia. No one is required to join us, but I beseech you all. Before long, Reagan's touch will reach us here in the safety of Raudur as it already has in Eldfal ... unless we stop her now. I've been her prisoner. I know how ruthless she is. She will stop at nothing to claim the power she feels she deserves, and she will use Callum as a weapon until she no longer needs him—until Iskalt belongs to her. Don't let her do to this city what she's done in Iskalt and now Eldfal, which stands no more. Put the call out to your friends and family. Let everyone know the time has come for the Raudur militia to take up arms to aid the future king of Iskalt. That man right there." Brea pointed at Lochlan. "He is the greatest ally Eldur will ever have, and he needs us to stand with him.

"I am just a simple girl from humble roots, despite my royal title. I understand you all have families and livelihoods you cannot abandon so easily. I stand with Lord Lochlan O'Shea, and I will fight by his side for the safety of all fae, no matter what kind of magic they possess, no matter what realm they call home. I ask you all to do the same. Send out the call to all of Eldur as your queen has requested. Join us, and together with Iskalt under King Lochlan's rule, Reagan will never stand a chance." Brea shuffled her feet in the silence that followed. "That's all I had to say, so ... uh, thank you for listening." Her cheeks flushed pink as the crowed cheered for her.

Lochlan was ready to follow Brea to the ends of the

world and back again. He couldn't imagine anyone who listened to her heartfelt pleas wouldn't feel the same. She thought she was an inept human. She didn't see the inner strength that called out to her people. She was a natural, and he owed her a debt he wasn't sure he could ever repay.

It took Lochlan and the queen two days to rally four-hundred volunteer militia from all across Eldur. It took Brea four hours to call in a thousand from the city's militia in their own backyard. He could kiss the ground she walked on.

"She did it." Finn shook his head in disbelief, staring down at the latest lists. "In one afternoon, she handed you an army."

"She'll make an excellent queen someday," Lochlan agreed.

"You know what this means, don't you?" Finn gave him a hard look. "You don't need to spend the next six months campaigning across Iskalt, calling for soldiers to join you. With nearly two thousand soldiers at your back now, you can make a move against Callum."

"I'd like to double that number with some of my own countrymen, but that can be done along the way." Lochlan was grateful for his friend's support. No matter what happened in Iskalt, Finn would have his back the whole way. He couldn't face this without the man who'd become more of a brother to him than his own flesh and blood.

"Pardon, Lord Lochlan," a page murmured behind them

in the throne room. The queen was busy handing out orders to prepare for such a huge response to Brea's rally cry. Lochlan suspected she was more than just proud of her daughter. She was speechless from the outpouring of support she'd garnered for Lochlan. "I've a message for you and Princess Brea. Could you see she gets it?" The boy gave a curt bow and handed over a letter sealed with the unmistakable twisted branches of Queen Reagan's seal—addressed to Lochlan O'Shea and Brea Robinson.

"What could she possibly have to say to you or Brea?" Finn frowned as Lochlan broke the seal.

Lochlan muttered a string of curses as he read the queen's missive. Part of him wanted to burn the letter and pretend he'd never seen it. But she deserved to know the truth. He'd seen what happened when Brea was kept in the dark, and he wouldn't be another attempting to manipulate her. "She needs to see this." He folded the letter and tucked it into his pocket. "Keep working on readying the campaign. I'll be back as soon as I can."

Lochlan knew where to find Brea during the hottest part of the day. She'd spent her morning at the stables before delivering her speech. No doubt she was exhausted. Heading to her rooms, he debated how to break the news.

He knocked on her door, but she didn't answer. Peeking in, he didn't see her. If he didn't know her as well as he did, he'd think someone had ransacked her room. Clothes lay scattered about, and half-empty teacups held the dregs of her morning and afternoon tea. She'd refused to let Rowena clean her room everyday, only letting her in at the end of the week to 'tidy up.' From what Lochlan had heard, Rowena crept into her rooms while the princess was busy with her horses. Otherwise, Lochlan wasn't sure Brea would have been able to find her bed.

"Brea?" He tapped on the door to the grotto. He didn't want to wake her if she was napping, but this was urgent. She lay sprawled on the chaise lounge in the cool darkness of the room. Her brown hair fanned out around her, and her cheeks flushed pink with sleep. She looked so peaceful he didn't want to bother her. She wore one of her simple tunics she'd no doubt purchased in the free marketplace—and nothing else. Her bare legs curled up as she lay on her side.

Sitting beside her, Lochlan called her name again, gently shaking her shoulder.

"What's happening? Who's there? I'm up." She tried to sit up but knocked her head against Lochlan's.

"Ouch." He rubbed his forehead, a smile tugging at his lips. She was a bewildered mess, not quite awake yet.

"Loch?" She scowled up at him. "It's the middle of the night. What do you want?"

"It's afternoon, and I spoke to you not four hours ago. Have you been asleep all this time?"

"It appears I don't know how to nap." Brea rubbed the sleep from her eyes. "I don't do quick little power naps. If I lay down, I'm out for a few hours at least. I don't usually fall asleep when I come in here."

"Listen to your body, Brea. Rest when you need it. We have a long campaign ahead of us."

"How's it going with the volunteers? Has my speech helped? It's probably too early to tell."

"You've performed a miracle, Brea." Lochlan brushed his fingertips along the edge of her face, wishing he could just focus on the success of her speech and not the news he brought with him. "A thousand city militia have volunteered since this afternoon."

"Shut up!" A smile unlike any he'd ever seen lit her face. "That's incredible."

"You're incredible." He tucked a stray curl behind her ear.

"Is that what you came to tell me? We should celebrate."

"I have news from Regan." He reluctantly pulled the envelope from his pocket.

"Myles?" She sat up and snatched the letter from his hands.

"She's offering a trade. She will free Myles if you give yourself over to her."

Brea's eyes moved rapidly as she scanned the short missive. Her tears ran freely, each one a stab in the gut for Lochlan.

"You can't give her what she wants, Brea. I know you love Myles and you'd do anything to free him, but if you give yourself to her, you will never leave Gelsi again. You will be her creature forever, a plaything she will manipulate to get what she wants."

"It's Myles." The helpless tone of her voice nearly broke him. Brea was anything but helpless, though he knew exactly how she felt. He'd felt the same when he'd heard of Alona's capture.

"And she is using him against you in the worst possible way."

"Why did you even tell me?" She dropped the parchment, letting it flutter to the floor.

"Because you deserve the truth. I won't be another royal who uses you as a pawn, keeping you in the dark. This is your choice. I won't insult you by making it for you."

"She's torturing him." Brea threw her arms around Lochlan, her shoulders shaking with sobs.

He pulled her onto his lap, letting her rest her head on his shoulder as she cried for the boy who'd once been her whole world. In so many ways he was jealous of Myles. He had her heart in a way no one else ever would.

"I know you don't want to hear this, Brea, but sometimes as a royal, we have to make hard decisions. Decisions that will benefit our people at great cost to ourselves. If Regan gets you within her grasp again, it won't end well for any of us. Least of all you."

"You think I care what she does to me? When I can free Myles in an instant? I don't care if she tosses me in the dungeon and throws away the key. I don't care if she marries me off to Griff so my children can be her blood heirs. Not if it means I can send Myles back home to his family where he can be safe."

The thought of Griffin married to Brea made Lochlan physically ill. He tightened his arms around her, wishing he could just hold onto her and keep her safe. But Brea didn't need or want anyone to protect her. She would see it as the ultimate betrayal. He would have to be true to his word and let her make this choice on her own. He just hoped she made the right one.

"You are too important to lose, Brea. Too important to Eldur. Too important to Fargelsi. And far too important to me."

Too important.

Brea didn't want to be important.

She wanted to be an impetuous teenager who didn't have to concern herself with the consequences of her actions. Well, she had the teenager thing down, considering she'd stomped from her own room leaving Lochlan calling after her.

She hadn't even been able to muster up the pride she should have felt when she managed to throw up a barrier across her doorway, locking him in.

Ha! He wouldn't be able to get out until his magic returned with the moon.

Sometimes there were benefits to this magic business. Other times, she wished she could flush it all away.

The full force of the Eldurian afternoon sun struck her

in the face as she stepped out from under the covered walkway to reach the fountain she now claimed as her own.

The coins representing every unfulfilled wish she'd cast since arriving glittered in the crystal-clear water.

"I'm not making a wish," she mumbled to herself. They only provided a false hope that any of this would ever get better.

While she was inspiring the people of Eldur and living in a grand palace, Myles was being tortured, and it was all her fault.

Yes, yes, she knew guilt was a useless emotion, but she clung to the desperation choking her, and she couldn't breathe.

She bent over, trying to catch her breath and rested a hand on the fountain. These waters weren't like those of Gelsi where creatures threatened to pull her under, but they held dangers all the same because they made her believe in something, even if it was a false belief.

Ripping her hand free, she slammed her foot against the stone. When it didn't hurt, she did it again.

"These stupid boots," she screamed, needing something, anything, to take the brunt of her anger. They wouldn't even let her stub her toe.

She slid to the ground and pressed her back up against the stone as hot tears burned her eyes. Myles' smiling face filled every space in her mind. He'd once been all she had. How could she let Regan keep him in her clutches?

Her mother might have been family by blood, but Myles was family by experience. He'd been there for everything.

Lochlan was cracked if he thought being a royal and making hard decisions meant anything to her compared to Myles.

She didn't know how long she sat there alone before the light faded away. "Dusk," she whispered.

And that meant... she felt his presence before she saw him.

Lochlan was like a single life raft in a crashing sea. Even if they disagreed on this, even if he'd never understand, she needed someone to see her, Brea Robinson, not the princess for just one moment.

Because the princess wanted to ride by Lochlan's side as he fought for his kingdom. She wanted to sit atop a beautiful horse at the head of the army that came for love and honor, not obligation. Tomorrow, when the gates of the Eldurian palace closed behind the last soldier, the princess of both Eldur and Fargelsi should be with them.

But Brea? The changeling girl raised as a human with a single friend to call her own knew what she needed to do.

Lochlan walked forward and slid down to sit at her side, his shoulder brushed hers as he leaned back against the raised wall of the fountain.

"How'd you find me?" she asked.

Lochlan's entire body was still, and he didn't answer her question. "Three years ago I went into the human realm of my own accord. Your mother didn't send me that time, but it had been months since I'd laid eyes on you. In the time I was away, you'd turned fifteen, but you were so much older than that. I saw it in your eyes."

He scrubbed a hand over his face, and Brea couldn't look at him. It had stopped feeling strange, knowing he'd watched over her for so many years. He was like a guardian angel, someone who'd been there when she thought she'd had few who cared.

Lochlan blew out a breath before continuing. "I went to the usual places to search for you. Your farm, your school. I didn't find you, and I started to panic."

"You were worried about me? Loch, you didn't know me. We'd never even spoken."

"Part of it was because I never wanted to have to tell your mothers anything happened to you, but there was more. I needed you to be okay. Me. Not your mothers."

"So, what happened?" she whispered, drying her tears with the sleeve of her tunic. "Was I okay?"

"No. I didn't see you at your farm, but there was a boy there. He was sitting under the tree where I'd seen you and him a hundred times before."

"Myles." A fresh batch of tears drifted down over her cheeks.

"Fae are not allowed to reveal themselves to humans. I didn't have any glamour magic to cover my features because it was daylight, but I couldn't help myself. I broke one of the most sacred laws of our world because I needed to know where you were."

"Wait." Brea turned her entire body toward him. "Are you saying you met Myles?"

"To his credit, he didn't seem scared of me. I think he was too distraught for that. I asked where the owners of that farm were, and he told me they were taking their daughter to an institution for the mentally unstable."

Brea shifted away from him, shame filling her.

"Don't hide from me, Brea." He lifted her chin so she met his gaze. "That boy... I mean... he was waiting to confront your parents. That's why he was there. He was ready to go to battle for you, do whatever was necessary. He's the only human I've ever actually liked."

"Hey." She pinched his side.

"You aren't human, Brea. And Alona was raised fae."

Brea couldn't wrap her head around everything he was saying. "So, Myles knew? About fae?"

"Not completely. He knew I was something other than human."

"That's why..." The breath rushed out of her as everything made sense. Myles never questioned what everyone else called her hallucinations. "He knew I wasn't crazy." She'd always thought he just didn't care if his best friend had delusions, that he was too kind to hold it against her. This changed everything. "Why are you telling me this?"

"Because, Brea, tomorrow I leave to fight for my throne, and I want you with me."

"But I'm a crap fighter."

"I know."

"I can't control my magic."

"Everyone knows that."

"Then why does it matter what I do? If I accept Regan's deal, it will have no impact on your campaign."

He pinned her with a look, his icy eyes swirling with

magic. "You do not know your worth, Brea. You will have an impact on me." He leaned closer, his voice dropping to a whisper. "You've always had an impact on me."

Brea closed the remaining distance, sealing her lips to his, reveling in the way his cold magic mingled with the heat of hers.

This kiss wasn't the first they'd shared. The first was nothing more than a ploy to make her angry.

The second only a moment born out of fear for what they were to discover the next day in Iskalt.

But this... she poured everything into the moment, wishing it didn't have to end. She'd known so many lies in the fae world that it was hard to determine fact from fiction.

Brea Robinson is a lie.

The old feeling crept up in her, because for once, she had no doubt Lochlan gave her all his truths. This time, she was the liar.

Desperation clung to them as Brea pushed Lochlan back into her room. A smile curved his lips, but smiles didn't belong to a night like this.

The night before the heir to the Iskalt throne left to reclaim his home.

The night before a princess of two kingdoms became a prisoner once again.

"Brea." Lochlan tried to stop her, but she cut off his words with another kiss, and his strength waned as he pulled her tighter against him, his large hands gripped her back as if she'd disappear the moment he let her go.

Brea hadn't given him the answer he wanted about leaving, not yet. But she'd made up her mind. Tears clouded her visions, and she squeezed her eyes shut, kissing Lochlan with everything she had.

His legs hit the bed, and he sat on the edge.

Brea hovered over him, opening her eyes to gaze into the depths of the man before her. He was beautiful in a way she'd never seen before. Also stubborn and kind of a jerk.

But there was nothing she wished for more than to stay in this spot in time forever.

Her heart hammered in her chest as she blinked tears away.

Lochlan reached up, brushing his thumb under her eye. "I'm going to make you a promise, Brea."

She shook her head, remembering Griff and his broken promises. "Don't, Loch. If you promise nothing, you break nothing."

A crease formed between his brows. "We will save Myles and Alona. I refuse to let you tell me to hold that promise back. Come with me into Iskalt where we will defeat my uncle. Then, with the might of Eldur and Iskalt combined, we will help them. I'll do anything to bring them back, Brea. Anything except losing you. If you go into that palace in Fargelsi, you will never walk out again. That isn't the way."

She pressed a finger to his lips, not wanting him to say another word. Myles might not be able to wait for them to conquer Iskalt, and if she lost him, she'd no longer be whole.

"Kiss me," she whispered. "Kiss me like tomorrow might never come. Make me think of nothing else. Please."

Sliding a hand around her back, he pulled her onto his lap, his eyes never leaving hers. "Don't be afraid of tomorrow, Brea. The dawn always follows the darkness."

"I didn't ask you to speak." She pushed him down onto the bed. "I told you to make me forget." Not waiting for him, she pressed her lips to his, sinking into him.

The fire that had burned between them since the day they met, the anger and defiance, expanded into an inferno as they both tried to take everything from the other.

When Lochlan slid a hand under her tunic, grazing the smooth skin of her stomach, his touch seared into her, and she needed more.

Sliding the shirt off over her head, she gazed down at him and cut off his protest with another kiss. It wasn't the time for proprieties he wouldn't have considered with any other fae woman.

She no longer wanted to be put on a pedestal while the fae world around her turned in a haze of immodesty and passion.

"Lochlan." She brought her lips to his ears. "We go to battle soon. Act like it."

His expression was hard as stone, and Brea waited for him to reject her, to tell her this wasn't right.

But it was. She just needed him to see it. They were both hurting and desperate, but out of all the decisions she second guessed and doubted, this one was as clear as the waters of her fountain.

She'd fought it, fought him, not willing to trust another O'Shea brother, but she couldn't deny it any longer.

"I want you." She skimmed her lips up over his cheek. "Tell me you want me too."

Lochlan gripped her hips and flipped her off him. She yelped as her back hit the bed. He held himself above her and dipped his head, capturing her lips. "We leave for battle tomorrow." He repeated her own words. He just didn't know they'd be headed toward two separate battles.

But he would, and she couldn't help but wonder if he'd ever forgive her.

Probably not.

This night might be all they ever had, and she was going to hold onto it, letting it be what she remembered as she became a prisoner once more.

Brea stared up into the canopy overhead as she let herself live in this dream world for a moment longer. As soon as she scooted out from under Lochlan's arm and left the bed behind, this reality would crack, never to be the same again.

Even if she somehow ended up back here at the Eldur palace, it would be after she'd betrayed them. She was supposedly some magical weapon that could be used against Regan, but underneath all of this fae mumbo-jumbo, everything in her still felt very much human.

And humans fought for those they loved.

He knew.

How had Myles known that her hallucinations were real and never told her? As they lay awake talking through most of the night, Lochlan explained how he'd told Myles Brea's life would be in danger if she learned the truth.

Which was just more proof of what she needed to do. Myles had done all he could to keep her safe. Now it was her turn.

Turning her head to the side, she studied the man beside her, the one she'd tried so hard to hate. Blond hair lay skewed across his forehead. She'd give anything to see those icy blue eyes once more, but if he woke, he'd never let her go.

And she had to do this.

There were no more tears, not anymore. Now was a time for decision, not emotion.

Lochlan grumbled as Brea rolled his arm off her and climbed out of the bed. Padding across the room, she pulled on the leather-patched riding pants Rowena never let her wear and a long tunic-shirt she belted at the waist. After slipping into her boots and packing a few supplies in a drawstring linen bag, she gripped the door handle.

Glancing back over her shoulder one final time, she hardened her resolve and hiked the bag onto her shoulder.

One day, she hoped he'd understand.

The door creaked when she opened it, and she slipped into the hall. The sun hadn't yet risen on Eldur, so most of the palace slept still. The sound of boots on stone echoed down the hall, and she ducked into an alcove to avoid being seen by the guard. Once he turned down another hall, she darted out and ran through the royal residence, not slowing until she was out in the main palace. A few servants prepared the main rooms for a new day. She passed the kitchens where the palace cooks had begun their morning routines.

Slipping into the front courtyard, Brea nodded to the guards on duty. They acknowledged her, but didn't speak. In these clothes with a hat on her head, they probably mistook her for a servant boy.

She wedged open a door to the palace rooms across the courtyard where the guard slept in shoebox rooms that were smaller than her bathtub.

By the time she reached her destination, she was already panting. Lifting her hand to the cracked wood, she knocked as quietly as she could.

No one came.

She knocked again and still, he didn't answer. Trying the door, she found the room empty, and something inside her deflated.

Only one person would help her get to Fargelsi, and he'd already left.

Turning on her heel, she headed back to the main palace, ready to slink back into her rooms, defeated. She'd barely made it out of Gelsi alive the first time. If she tried the journey on her own, she'd surely die, and what good would that do Myles?

She passed the small courtyard near her rooms where the fountain had been her constant companion and froze. Pivoting toward the fountain, she took in the man standing in front of it with his sword belt on and a bag at his feet.

"Finn?"

He turned toward her. "I've been waiting out here. I didn't want to miss you."

She choked back a sob. When she'd knocked on his door and found him gone, she thought she'd lost before she began. "How did you know?"

He stepped toward her. "I was with Loch when he received the message." His eyes found hers. "If it was Alona, I'd go."

That was her answer. This was the right thing. "And you what? Packed me some supplies?" She grinned

"Don't be a fool, Brea. Without control of your magic, you'd never make it back through the Vatlands. Have you forgotten the state we found you in last time?"

She couldn't let herself hope. "You're—"

"Coming with you. Yes. I'll get you to Fargelsi."

"I could kiss you right now." The fear inside her receded and for the first time, she truly thought she could save Myles.

"Please don't. I'm already betraying Loch. I won't make it worse by kissing the woman he loves."

"He doesn't love me," she scoffed, trying to ignore the other part of what he'd said. Finn was right. Lochlan would see this as a betrayal. In one night, he'd lose both her and his best friend.

"Brea." He held her gaze. "He has been in love with you since before you knew he existed."

It was too much information for her already-overloaded brain. Lochlan loved her now, but that love would shatter into a million pieces when he woke to find her gone.

"I cannot handle anything more than this mission." She

released a sigh as her eyes memorized every stone of her favorite place in the palace. Would she ever see them again?

Finn wrapped an arm around her shoulders. "You'll come back, Brea. We'll make sure of it."

She wished she had so much faith. Fishing a copper coin from the pouch at her waist, she stepped up to the fountain one final time.

When the sun rose, Lochlan would ride into Iskalt with nothing more than militia at his back.

Maybe they were both doing what they'd always been meant for. Brea was a Fargelsian princess just as much as an Eldurian one. She only had to accept that.

Pressing her lips to the coin, she let it fly toward the water, closing her eyes as it disappeared under the ripples.

"Keep him safe," she whispered. "Keep them all safe."

With one last sweep of her eyes, she followed Finn through the palace to the path that would take them to the stables.

Finn saddled two horses as Brea looked back at the shining palace, standing like a beacon of the goodness she'd experienced for the first time in her life. She'd hold it in her heart to keep the dark away.

She mounted Sassa, the same horse that had taken her to catch Lochlan on the way to Iskalt.

Leaning forward, she patted her neck. "Ready for another adventure?"

The twin ponies stood in their stall, watching Brea leave them behind. She'd never forget everything she'd experienced here.

"Here." Finn held a knife and scabbard toward her. "You're going to need this."

She nodded and took the blade, strapping it to her leg. Shifting in the saddle, she sat up straighter. "For Myles."

He nodded. "And Alona."

Brea hesitated. "I will try to help her too. You know that, right?"

"Yes, Brea. I know." He clicked his tongue, nudging the horse forward. The only stable boy awake ran after them as soon as he noticed them, but there was no stopping Brea now.

When the dawn finally appeared, the palace that had finally started to feel like home was nothing more than a structure in the distance, indistinguishable and unremarkable.

Brea knew differently. Eldur and the people she'd come to love would carry the hope for this realm, but it was time for her to leave hope behind.

Lochlan knew Brea was gone the moment he woke. It was like he felt it in his soul.

Everything in him screamed to race after her, knowing she couldn't have gotten far, but she'd made this choice. Who was he to unmake it?

Lochlan tore through his room under the guise of preparing for his journey. Really, he just wanted to throw things. A teacup shattered against the wall, sending a spray of tiny glass shards cascading down the stone.

Someone knocked on his door, but he couldn't see anyone, not until he got his emotions under control. At least it was daylight so his magic couldn't spin out of control.

"Lochlan O'Shea." The voice reverberated around the room, and he closed his eyes, knowing that tone all too well.

"She's gone, Tierney." Everyone knew Tierney as the

sweet foil to the harder Faolan, but Lochlan knew better. Growing up, she'd been the one punishing him and Alona for their constant schemes while her wife was embroiled in affairs of the kingdom.

Both the Eldurian women loved him like their own son, but it was Tierney who raised him.

"Loch, we've heard reports of crashes coming from this room. The guards are afraid to enter." Her eyes drifted around the disheveled room. "Hmm... Whatever has happened cannot warrant a tantrum on the morning you leave for Iskalt."

"I'm not throwing a tantrum," he grumbled.

"Aren't you?" One eyebrow raised, she approached him and reached her slender arms out to pull him into a hug just as she'd done a thousand times over the years.

He let her hold him only a moment before pulling away. Not only had Brea left on the eve of their departure, she hadn't told her mothers, the two women who'd be crushed by her willingness to disappear into Regan's household once more.

"Now," Tierney said calmly. "Tell me what has ruffled the feathers of the inscrutable Iskalt king." She'd always called him the king instead of simply a prince despite the fact that he didn't wear the crown.

"Brea." Call him a coward, but he couldn't meet her eyes as he told her the news. "She has left for Fargelsi."

Tierney stepped back, her face impassive as she took in the news. She sucked in a breath and turned to the door. "Guard, please inform the queen she is needed in the throne room and then fetch Finnegan Donovan. He will have had something to do with this."

Lochlan didn't know how she could be so calm when he'd just told her Brea was on her way to the enemy.

"Get mad," he said. "Come on, Tierney. I know this calm facade is only for show. I've seen your temper. Throw something. Curse the human world that made Brea so self-righteous."

Tierney turned back toward him. "You have done enough of that for the both of us, wouldn't you say? Now, I must walk to the throne room to tell my wife another daughter of ours will soon be in the hands of her enemy. I know you, and I know her. One of the three of us must keep our heads. Come. You have a lot of explaining to do, boy."

Lochlan took in the mess he'd made, knowing it would be cleaned by the time he returned. And then, when the sun rose directly over Eldur, he'd lead his makeshift army away from the only home he could remember in any detail.

Brea leaving didn't change his duty to his people.

Faolan paced the length of the throne room when they arrived, tears already staining her cheeks.

She knew.

When she saw them, she rushed forward. "Where is my daughter?"

Lochlan let them yell at him, he let Faolan rant. He deserved it, after all.

"When a messenger from a foreign queen comes to this palace, Lochlan, no one sees them before me." Faolan was practically growling now. "How dare you make decisions about my kingdom, my daughter."

"She deserved—"

Faolan cut him off. "That isn't for you to decide! The Iskalt throne might rightfully be yours, but I am the Queen of Eldur. My word in this palace must be obeyed." Her lips formed a sneer. "She never should have seen that message or had that choice before her."

Lochlan couldn't take this any longer. He'd never known Faolan to be particularly kind, but this went too far, even for her. "You would have me lie to your daughter?" As much as he hated the choice she'd made, he never questioned if showing Brea the message was the right thing to do.

"Yes!" Faolan's screech grated on his nerves. "We are fae, Lochlan. I don't care if we aren't the tricksters of Fargelsi, lies are still currency here. We aren't ruled by human morality. Maybe you've spent too much time in the human world or trapped in those human books over the years."

A throat cleared from the doorway, and a young guard stepped in. "Your Majesty." He bowed.

"What is it?" she snapped.

"Finnegan Donovan could not be found. His room is empty, and no one has seen him yet this morning."

Lochlan closed his eyes for a brief moment, knowing exactly where his best friend had gone. "He took Brea to Fargelsi."

Tierney looked to the guard. "You can go. Please inform

the militia generals to prepare their men for departure." It was an order Lochlan should have given, but as he stood in his stand-off with Faolan, he couldn't think of his next moves.

The guard left them alone once again.

"Finn." Faolan cursed. "That boy has always been trouble."

"Trouble," Lochlan scoffed. "Was he trouble when he helped save Brea from the Vatlands all those months ago? Or when he saved my life along the Fargelsi border? What about when he rode by my side to investigate the village in Iskalt—something you were against."

He pictured Brea traveling the swampy Vatlands with all number of creatures keeping her company, not to mention the mud pits. "She's going to live because of Finn." It didn't make the betrayal sting any less. Would Brea have stayed if she didn't have someone to lead her on the treacherous journey? Not likely.

"Watch what you say next, young man." Faolan's face held a storm Lochlan no longer cared if he unleashed. If she had her way, he'd be no better than Griff was to Brea, a lying, conniving fae—not unlike those in the human storybooks.

"I won't let you turn me in to her enemy." He didn't agree with her choice and wouldn't get past the betrayal any time soon, but he would always choose Brea's side.

"She wanted this." Faolan's ranting started to make less and less sense. "To return to Regan."

"What are you talking about?" Lochlan burned with anger.

"Faolan." Tierney put a hand on her back, and the queen instantly relaxed. "Brea did what she thought right."

"Yes, Yes." Faolan covered her face in her hands, her back shaking. "I know." She sniffed. "I'm sorry."

Lochlan couldn't remember ever seeing Faolan cry. If Finn were here, he'd hug the queen, despite it being wildly inappropriate for a mere soldier. He wouldn't have cared.

How was Lochlan supposed to ride to reclaim his kingdom without the two people who got him to this point? He wouldn't have the courage without Finn or the army and the inspiration without Brea.

"I couldn't protect either of them," Faolan cried as her wife rubbed her back.

Lochlan glanced from the queen to the door. The only thing that would fill the Brea-sized hole in his chest was looking out on the men and women volunteering to ride into Iskalt.

Tierney's glassy eyes met his, and she nodded, giving him permission to leave. There'd be no regal goodbyes, no tearful moments for him.

When he stepped into the hall, a voice called him back. "Lochlan." Faolan ran after him. "Go with the best wishes of Eldur. But come back to us. Please."

He couldn't promise his return, so he dipped into a bow. It wasn't out of obligation, it never had been. A king didn't bow to other royals. But she'd taken him in when he had nothing. There were few people he loved or respected as much as Faolan and Tierney Cahill.

Clearing his throat, he turned and walked away from the throne room and the people in it.

He reached the armory where a servant met him with the bag he'd left in his rooms. If he succeeded, they may never be his rooms again. And if he failed, they might still not belong to him.

After all, dead men needed no beds.

He refused to stop fighting for his people while there was breath in his lungs.

In that way, he understood Brea's sacrifice. To her, Myles was her world, just like Iskalt was his.

He strapped a sword belt around his waist and drew the sword, peering at his reflection in the gleaming blade. The man staring back at him wasn't the boy who'd come to Eldur as a ward of the crown, an orphan kid whose own brother would grow to hate him.

No, the hard eyes meeting his were those of someone who had nothing left to lose.

He slid the blade into its scabbard and wrapped his fingers around the smooth wood of his bow. Slinging a quiver of arrows over one shoulder, he left to meet his soldiers.

Some gathered in the courtyard just inside the gates. Others congregated in the streets between the palace and the stables.

Master Arturo himself brought Lochlan's horse forward and held him steady as Lochlan mounted the great warbeast. He'd always thought the world looked different from atop a horse, smaller somehow.

And with a sword at one's waist, it became a crueler place.

Maybe Faolan was right. Being cruel was in a fae's nature, lying a part of who they were.

He'd told Brea the truth, and it might get her killed—if she were lucky.

Finn knew the truth and had betrayed Lochlan for it.

It was time for him to erase silly human notions and give in to what he'd always been meant to be.

An ice king.

Brea never wanted to see the southern Vatlands marshes again. She never wanted to feel the squish of mud under her boots, see a snake or hear the croak of a frog for the rest of her life, no matter how long that might be.

With solid ground beneath her once more, she gazed at the long winding road that would lead to the palace where her aunt reigned. A troop of guards awaited her, having already informed her Regan reinforced the border so none could cross without permission, not just those with Fargelsian blood anymore.

"This is where I have to leave you." Finn stood in the mud up to his knees.

"I wish you could cross the border with me." Regan would never let him cross.

"I'd give anything to get inside that dungeon to see Alona again."

"I have a feeling I'll be right there with her in a few hours."

"Give her a message for me?" Finn asked.

"Of course."

"Tell her I've never stopped thinking of her."

"I'll do everything I can for her." Brea gave him a last farewell before they headed in opposite directions. Finn would travel along the Gelsi border until he found Faolan's army, and he would do his part to bring down the barrier that kept him out.

Brea traveled this road once before with Neeve. It felt like another lifetime—something that happened to another version of herself.

It took her and the guards all night to reach the outskirts of the forest city that surrounded the palace. Her companions refused to speak to her, but they didn't let her out of their sight. Regan knew she would come. She'd had her people waiting.

Months ago, Brea was on horseback making this journey. This time, she relied on her own two feet to follow the guards' horses. They didn't offer her a ride. She'd been terrified escaping Fargelsi, but there'd also been hope of something good at the end of the road.

Now, only darkness and imprisonment awaited her.

Her time in Eldur had changed her. She was stronger. More confident, and so very angry with her aunt. She wished she could walk into the palace and toss her aunt in the dungeon she was so fond of. Brea might possess the power to defeat her ... someday, but Myles didn't have time to wait around for someday to arrive. He needed her now.

Brea followed the guards down the high road to the main bridge that would lead them directly to the palace. They made it as far as the front gate before the palace guards stopped them.

"What do you bring us?" one of them asked the men on horseback.

He started to speak, but Brea cut him off. "I'm here to see the queen."

"What do you think this is? Eldur? The guard snorted. "Go back where you came from, peasant."

"She's requested my presence." Brea stood firmly.

"Has she, now?" The man barked out a laugh and spit at Brea's feet. He looked to the guards and they nodded, confirming Brea's words.

"She won't like it if you turn her niece away. I've had a long trip from Eldur, and I'd like to retire to my rooms."

"Brea?"

His voice shouldn't still affect her. Not after all this time and the gravity of his betrayal.

"Griffin." Brea was proud of her calm tone, not betraying her feelings.

"I will escort the queen's niece to her rooms." Griff shouldered past the guards, taking her hand in his like it was old times.

Brea tugged her hand away, and without another word, followed him into the palace.

"I would see her now to get this over with," Brea said, hesitating at the foot of the stairs. "I won't be spending the night in my old rooms. I'm here to trade myself for Myles. I'm sure you're aware of your queen's offer. It was likely your idea to bring him here. You'd know I'd do anything for him, and you used it against me."

"Brea." He looked haggard and so very tired. "Nothing is as it seems here."

"You're the one who taught me that." Brea took the steps up to the queen's quarters, not waiting for Griff to show her the way.

"You should wait to see her in the morning. Give her a chance to call for you when she's ready."

"I'm over it. I'm so over Regan and the intimidation she exudes, her endless parties and her syrupy sweet facade. We do this my way. She made me an offer, and I'm here to accept it on my terms."

Griff rushed up the stairs behind her.

She found her aunt on the terrace, just like any other day. She was lingering over her breakfast, reading reports of the goings on in Gelsi. Somewhere in that stack of papers there was likely a form briefing the queen of the Eldur troops working tirelessly to bring down her border spell. Another one detailing the movements of the young Iskalt king, and probably another one telling her Brea had arrived.

Brea slammed the missive she'd received from Regan on the table in front of the queen.

"Brea, darling." Regan beamed her beautiful, perfect white smile at her. "You've been a naughty girl." She eyed the mud-stained clothes she still wore from her trek across the Vatlands.

"Cut the crap, Regan." Brea collapsed on the delicate vine chair opposite her aunt. She used to be afraid she'd break her aunt's chairs, but she understood magic better now. "You made me an offer. I'm here to accept it on a few conditions."

"Oh, come now. Let's catch up before we discuss unpleasant things."

"I don't have it in me." Brea wiped a tired hand over her eyes. "Just drop the pretense, and let's get down to brass tacks."

"Oh, I missed your charming human phrases, dear. It's been so quiet here without you. Would you like some tea?" She rang for her maid.

Brea turned, hoping to see Neeve again, but frowned when one of the triplets dropped into a curtsy before the queen.

"Where is Neeve?" Brea frowned.

"She's been ... detained. Punishment for helping you escape, I'm afraid." Regan had the triplet pour her a cup of hot herbal tea, but Brea didn't trust anything her aunt had a hand in making. "She's faring much better than that friend of hers from the village."

Brea's eyes widened. "Moria?"

"Yes, that was her name. A nasty business, executions."

Her blood froze in her veins. Moira was dead. Guilt and sadness warred inside her. And Neeve was suffering her grief in the dungeons.

"Drink up, dear, and tell me all about your time in Eldur. Wasn't it just dreadful under that hot and unforgiving sun?" Regan leaned forward as if preparing for a grand story.

Brea's gaze narrowed. "Fine, I'll make you a counter offer if you're just going to simper at me all morning." She sucked in a breath. She had to get Neeve out of there. After Moira, she owed it to her. "I'm here. Release Myles and Alona ... Neeve too. Let them go, and I will stay." She threw a look to Griff. "Release them and I will..." Pausing, she knew she'd regret the next words. "Marry Griff. Willingly. He can be the king, and I'll be your ornamental queen. If I ever have children, they will be your blood heirs." The prospect of such a life sickened her. She couldn't imagine a world where she would ever let Griffin touch her, much less father her children. Her mind instantly went to thoughts of Lochlan and of all the things they would never have together, and it took every bit of strength she possessed to keep the tears at bay.

"But if I do all of that, you have to take the barrier down and free your people.

"We'll, now, I see someone's been doing their homework since she ran away. But that's not going to happen. You will have to amend your terms, dear."

"Let's get to the part where you free my friends." She had to remind herself that was why she was here.

"Alona is your friend now?" Regan cocked her head at Brea. "A girl you've never even met."

"We have mutual friends we both care a great deal about." Brea leaned back in her seat, weary down to her bones.

"I'm afraid I can't release Alona. She is too important. Myles, even your little traitor friend, Neeve are nothing to me. Though clearly, they mean a great deal to you. You've come such a long way for them. Why not take the night to relax and enjoy your old rooms, and we can discuss this tomorrow when you're in a better mood."

"We'll discuss it now."

"Blast, you really are my brother's child. Just as stubborn and needlessly noble."

"That might be the best thing I've ever heard about my fae father." Though Brea knew precious little about the man Faolan agreed to have a weapon-child with. "Release Myles and Neeve today. Myles will go back to the human realm unharmed, and Neeve will be sent to the palace at Eldur."

"Fine." Regan waved a delicate hand. "Go to your rooms and get cleaned up. Your clothes are still in your wardrobe. We will have a party to celebrate your return tomorrow evening."

"No." Brea slammed her fist down on the table causing Regan to flinch. "I will not be your plaything or your paper doll to dress up when you're bored. And I sure as hell won't spend my life suffering through your parties. I am here to trade places with Myles. Period."

"You expect me to throw you in the dungeon like a useless human when you are to be queen one day?" Regan threw her head back and laughed. "No, darling, you are my prisoner, but I don't need iron bars and cells to keep you under control. You've proven just how malleable you can be. Myles will be freed from the dungeons, but he won't return to the human realm. He will take up residence at Griffin's cottage where Leith will serve as his warden. We'll even send Neeve there to keep house. They'll be safe and happy while you take up your role as my doting niece who has come home at last."

"I will agree to your terms, but I have terms of my own." Brea leaned forward. "I get to see Myles and Neeve before you send them to the cottage, *today.* And I get to visit them once a month."

"Absolutely not. I will not have my niece cavorting with prisoners. If you wish for them to be free, you will not speak to them. You will not see them. Those are the terms, dear. It is the best you will do."

"I will attend your parties, wear your ridiculous dresses and play whatever simpering idiot role you want of me. But every other day of my captivity, I don't see you, I don't talk to you, I don't even hear your voice. I will stay in my rooms, only visiting the gardens or the stables so I have something to do. I will wear whatever I want, and I will prepare my own food."

"You will eat a steady diet of Gelsi berries to subdue your magic."

"No." Brea refused to give her that much power. "I will honor our deal if you keep up your side of the bargain. If Myles is your leverage over me, then my magic is my leverage over you. This is about trust, Regan. You should give it a try. I'll give you everything you want, but you will not subdue my magic."

Lochlan gazed across the sprawling camp that grew in numbers everyday. A mishmash of Eldurians and his own countrymen and women. More than two thousand soldiers and militia had joined him in his march for the Iskalt palace. The Eldurians came because their princess asked them to, though they still didn't know Brea was theirs. The connection between her and her people was evident in the way they followed her lead.

He'd never had any doubt Brea could inspire people to greatness. But what astounded him were the sheer numbers of Iskalt men and women who joined them along their journey.

"Your Majesty." A young man several years younger than Lochlan approached his tent with a formal bow.

"Captain Walsh." Lochlan returned his bow with a nod. It was strange the way his countrymen treated him with such respect and reverence. It reminded him of the way his father's men behaved around the king. "How are your men faring this morning?"

"Very well, sire. We've scouted the roads around the palace and discovered a way around Callum's men."

"Show me on the map." Lochlan bent over the large map covering the makeshift table in his tent. Captain Walsh was the first man Lochlan met when he led his soldiers through the pass along the Northern Vatlands and into Iskalt near the village Callum slaughtered. The young man led a contingent of soldiers—boys mostly—who had heard Lochlan was coming. They claimed they wanted to join their rightful king and help him take his throne. Lochlan was speechless. Walsh led more than four hundred young soldiers, all eager to do their part.

"Excellent job, Walsh." Lochlan clapped him on the back, placing a marker on the map where he planned for his army to make a move on the palace.

"Thank you, sire." The captain bowed and took his leave, seeking out a hot meal and a warm bed after a long night of scouting.

A sense of pride swept through Lochlan. He was finally making a move to claim his throne. He had a capable army at his back, with day and night magic wielders. He'd never felt more certain of his path. Never felt so like the King of Iskalt he was born to be. And he'd never felt so alone.

Deep down, Lochlan understood why Finn left to put his efforts into freeing the woman he loved. He had no doubt, if given a chance to swap places with Alona, Finn would do it without a second thought. But Lochlan needed his best friend. Here among his soldiers, captains and lieutenants, Lochlan had no one he could trust the way he trusted Finn. He second guessed every decision he made, asking himself what Finn would say if he were here. He didn't want to resent his best friend for abandoning him at the worst possible time. He didn't want to resent him for doing what he had to for Alona. But he still felt the sting of betrayal every morning when he woke up in his tent alone without the one person he trusted above all others to advise him. Without Finn ... without his brother, Lochlan was lost.

"Your Highness?" An older man approached the tent.

Lochlan frowned. The man looked oddly familiar, but he couldn't place him. "You were one of my father's men?"

The man smiled, his eyes crinkling with amusement. "You used to call me uncle when you were just a boy." He held his hand out, and Lochlan took it, shaking his hand, but his name escaped him.

"Brennan Cormac," the man supplied.

"Of course." A genuine smile spread across Lochlan's face. "Uncle Bren." Lochlan remembered playing with Brennan's sons not long before his parents' deaths.

"I once served as a general in your father's army. I'm an old man now. Retired for twenty years since the wrong O'Shea thought to sit on your father's throne and send his boys off to grow up in foreign courts. I've waited for this day for a long time, your Majesty. I'd be proud to help Nial O'Shea's son take what belongs to him."

"I find myself surrounded by inexperienced soldiers and militia. I am in dire need of a seasoned advisor. I would be honored to work with the man my father called brother."

"He'd be damned proud of you, Lochlan."

"Thank you, sir." Lochlan stepped back, offering Brennan a seat by the table.

"Now, how can I help?"

It felt strange, trusting a man he barely remembered, but if his father trusted Brennan with his life, then Lochlan could too.

Nephew,

Go back to your Eldur queen and hide behind her skirts like you've been doing all your life. Your rag-tag unit of boys and farmers with pitchforks don't stand a chance against a king's army. Go home before you hurt yourself and get those good Iskalt boys killed playing war games you can't hope to win.

Your uncle,

Callum O'Shea, King of Iskalt

Lochlan crumpled the letter in his hand.

"You might as well wipe your rear with that. Nothing Callum has to say is worth the parchment it's written on."

Brennan studied the map of Iskalt in the growing darkness. Another day gone, and they hadn't made a move yet. Lochlan had spent the day with Brennan surveying his troops and making plans, but Lochlan still didn't feel confident about his chances against Callum's forces. His magic wielders alone could level Loch's army.

"You know what you have to do, Loch. It's the only clear path to victory."

Lochlan stared at the map, hoping to see whatever Brennan saw, but he just saw the makings of a bloody battle and terrible odds. "And what's that? Go home like my uncle told me to?"

Brennan snorted. "Of course not. Callum and all his advisors are as predictable as a textbook. They will not expect you to think outside the box."

"Make your suggestions." Lochlan gave him a curt nod to go on.

"Callum underestimates you. He sees you as a spoiled young prince. A boy with a streak of entitlement a mile wide. He doesn't know you, so let's catch him off guard."

"How?"

"You have something he doesn't. A thousand Eldurians with day magic. We attack at noon tomorrow. Your friends' fire magic will send Callum's soldiers running for cover. They'll never expect it."

"But with only a fraction of his numbers, all the fire magic in the world isn't going to help if we can't overcome his thousands. We would stand a better chance if we attack at dusk when my soldiers have both fire magic and ice magic."

"And Callum's thousands will also have their ice magic at the ready. But if we attack at noon, that puts all of Callum's men and your Iskalt soldiers on an even footing. At noon, they're all just men. Your fire magic wielders will give you the edge you need to get inside and overthrow that spineless coward once and for all. He's so arrogant and close-minded, he'll never see it coming. He would never consider not fighting with magic, and he will expect the same of you.

Lochlan studied the map and the numbers, pitting his army against Callum's larger one. It could be a suicide mission, but if Callum made certain assumptions and relied too heavily on his magic wielders, then pure brawn could work.

What would Finn say? He could practically hear Finn's excitement for this plan. He would appreciate the simplicity of it. Pitting soldiers against soldiers at a time when their ice magic lay dormant, leaving them with nothing but their swords and their wit. It would come down to who were the better fighters, and who wanted it more. He could feel the anticipation of his soldiers. They wanted this. Even the Eldurians were passionate about removing Callum O'Shea from his throne after what he did in Eldfal.

"We march at noon." He was ready for this. Lochlan O'Shea was borne to take this throne and repair the damage his uncle had wrought over the last two decades. It was time, and he was ready. As ready as he would be without the two most important people in his life who should be standing at his side.

"The men are in place, your Highness." Captain Walsh approached Lochlan and Brennan where they stood overlooking his army surrounding the Isklat palace. "Trebuchets and catapults are at the ready. We'll breach those high walls in no time, sire."

Lochlan frowned. Something wasn't right. Callum would never sit inside his castle while an army surrounded him. Siege wasn't his style. "He's not taking me seriously," Lochlan muttered.

"He doesn't believe we have a chance of defeating him during the day," Brennan said. "That mistake will lead to his demise."

"Walsh, have your men lay waste to those walls," Lochlan gave the order. "Brennan, call the longbowmen to cover them. This will be a long day, and we're up against more experienced men. We need to be smarter and faster."

"You can count on us, sire. We will have you on your throne by evening" Walsh gave a curt bow before he set off to give the order to begin the siege of Lochlan's ancestral home.

Within the first few hours, Lochlan knew this would not be a quick afternoon battle. He charged down the line on his black warhorse, calling out orders for his archers to engage the moment Callum's men made an appearance. As of yet, Callum hadn't even acknowledged Lochlan's siege. He threw everything they had at the palace walls, which were finally crumbling, but it would take most of the night to bring them down. His men were tired and tense from their one-sided battle. Soot streaked their faces as the ground shook from the catapults launching their burning missiles.

"He's toying with me." Lochlan rode beside one of his father's greatest friends, wondering if he'd made a mistake trusting in him.

"He thinks he will tire you out waiting for sunset."

"And he's right. Our soldiers have already had a long day. They cannot withstand a full night of this."

"The Eldurians will be our secret weapon," Brennan insisted. "They wait just over the next rise."

"Waiting for night? When they'll be as useless as we are right now?" Lochlan was losing patience after so many monotonous hours of the same activity.

"Waiting for the right moment to turn the tide in your favor, your Majesty. Callum has little mind for battle strategy. He will not make a move against you tonight. He's prepared to let us throw ourselves at this wall all night and maybe even the next until we are so exhausted we can't even think straight. That is when he will make his move. And that is when the Eldurians will defeat him."

"I see the sense of your plan." Lochlan gripped the reins of his horse tightly. "It is the waiting that is killing me. Waiting and worrying about my soldiers."

"We will rest the soldiers in shifts so they will be ready when the time is right. You are young, lad." Brennan laughed, slapping him on the back. "Too young to know how boring and miserable war can be. The heat of battle isn't always the hardest part. When it's just you and the blade in your hand, time flies. Nothing matters beyond the death of your immediate opponent and where the next one lies in wait. But siege? Siege is a different beast all together. Callum's advisors are making you wait just for that reason. They're not hiding behind these walls because they're scared. Callum is showing patience I didn't think he had. We will wait patiently, and when we lure him out, we will be ready."

"I appreciate your advice, Brennan." Lochlan nodded, watching as a fresh unit came to relieve the weary soldiers manning the trebuchets.

"I would have thought the Eldurian Queen would have sent you with some of her own advisors." Brennan glanced at Lochlan, trying to gauge his reaction to the prying question.

"She is supportive, but her attention is on Fargelsi. Until her daughter returns, Queen Faolan will not have much to offer Iskalt." It felt odd, explaining Lochlan's lack of support in the way of seasoned officers and commanders. His soldiers were green, and he had precious little experience himself.

"I imagine Eamon Donovan is banging at the Gelsi border much like we're doing with this wall. He will see Princess Alona home or die trying." Brennan sat up taller in his saddle. "It does my heart good to see a light at the end of the tunnel, my boy. You will make a king your father would be proud of. You'll restore the relationships between Iskalt and Eldur, and then we can focus on the real threat—bringing that Fargelsian witch down once and for all."

"That's the goal." Lochlan sighed. "Though I'm not sure I see the light yet."

"We've come a long way since you were a child, your Majesty. Just you wait. Your reign will be magnificent."

Lochlan wished he had Brennan's optimism. Without Finn, Alona and Brea, he felt like he was missing an arm. His confidence was gone, and he was lost in a sea of indecision and second-guessing himself.

Every morning that Brea woke in the extravagance of the Fargelsi palace was like fighting a new battle. Forcing herself to rise.

Facing the servants and guards acting as if she'd never left.

And Griff.

With a sigh, she eyed him where he sat across the room. "Are you watching me sleep? Again?" Every time she opened her eyes, the beautiful man she'd once thought she could love stared back at her.

"Just afraid you'll disappear on me." He stood and moved closer, his eyes never leaving her face.

Brea sat up and scooted back until she hit the headboard. "You're creepy. You shouldn't sneak into my room this early in the morning."

"Because you never crept into mine in the middle of the night?" One eyebrow arched, and Brea was hit with a wave of emotions and feelings, cutting the air off from her lungs.

She'd been happy. None of it was real, but it was the first time in her life she hadn't just had to accept her life. She'd enjoyed it. "Griff," she breathed.

"Number seven." He stepped closer to the bed. "That you don't fix your hair at every possible moment." He took a seat on the edge of the bed and reached out to tuck an errant strand behind her ear. "The other ladies of the court worry over their appearances, never leaving a single lock out of place. But you... Even after waking up with the most ridiculously messy hair... It doesn't bother you."

She gripped his wrist and forced it down, wanting to push him away, to tell him nothing he said had any effect on her. In a way, it didn't. She didn't love Griffin O'Shea, she knew that now. But his ten things he loved about her still made her heart skip a beat when most people couldn't even find one. "You missed seven."

He frowned. "I did not. Did you not receive my message?"

"What message?"

"Regan sent me to examine a rift in the barrier near the Northern Vatlands, but instead of a tear, I found Loch and his men."

She nodded, already knowing where this was going. "You were the one who told him Myles was here."

"I also gave him a sealed letter for you. In it was number seven."

Lochlan never mentioned a letter, but she couldn't muster the anger or indignation for him, not when he might be fighting for his life while she sat here with his brother. "What did it say?"

He slid from the bed. "I can't tell you now." He put a finger to his lips.

Brea followed his gaze around the room. She almost forgot her aunt could listen to any conversation that happened in here.

"I've missed you, Brea."

As she stared into his entrancing gaze, she realized she'd missed him too, but not the Griff who'd lied to her or allowed her to be her aunt's pawn.

She missed the guy racing horses across the open land near his cottage, the one with a smile in his eyes and laughter in his voice.

The man who'd made her feel safe when her entire world had been turned upside down.

That version of Griffin O'Shea didn't exist.

"Come here." His eyes pleaded with her.

Against her better judgement, she stood and approached him, letting him pull her into his familiar hug. She breathed in his scent, letting it calm her.

"Meet me in the stables in one hour," he whispered into her hair. "Please."

She nodded against him, not wanting to let go. No matter what Griff had done in the past or his loyalty to her aunt, when he walked out that door, she couldn't help feeling she'd be very much alone in this dangerous palace.

But she'd known from the moment she decided to take Regan's deal, she'd have to do this on her own. Save Myles. Marry Griff. Live her life as a prisoner.

He dropped his arms and stepped back, giving her one final imploring look before leaving her to the silence of her solitude. She flopped back onto her bed, staring into the vines creeping up the walls of the room.

If only Lochlan could see her now.

A few weeks ago, she'd laid beside him, knowing that their one night was the end of something that never really started. Where was he now? She had no doubt the people of Iskalt rose as their true king returned, but would it be enough?

It had to be.

If she was going to spend her life behind the walls of this palace, she had to believe he was out there conquering the world. That was who he was.

A tear raced down her cheek, but she wiped it away. There was no room in her heart for sadness, not when all she wanted was for it to harden into stone. Maybe then, none of this would hurt so much.

Heaving herself out of bed once more, she dressed in her faded leathers and tunic she'd arrived in that one of the triplets had washed. She refused to wear anything in her closet from before.

The guards on the bridge had taken her knife and never returned it. They couldn't have an angry armed princess running around the palace grounds. She kicked the empty sheath across the floor before stomping from the room, the clack of her Eldurian boots against the gleaming floors gave her some sense of satisfaction.

Guards and servants smiled at her as she passed, but just like everything in Fargelsi, there was a forced cheer behind it.

Her stomach rumbled, but she'd barely eaten in the days since she arrived, choosing to hole herself up in her room, sleeping the days away rather than make her way down to the kitchens to fend for herself. The first night at the celebration Regan ordered her to attend, she'd pilfered an unopen bottle of wine from the cellar and gotten sloppy drunk out of spite.

Since then, her aunt hadn't come to see her, which was fine with Brea.

No one stopped her on the way across the falls to the stables, and as she entered, a familiar scent struck her, reminding her of Master Arturo and the ponies. She'd grown to love her life in Eldur, and then it was all torn away.

But she didn't regret it. Not now that Myles and Neeve were safe.

"Brea," Griff hissed, poking his head out from one of the stalls.

She jumped, slapping a hand to her chest. "Are you trying to kill me? Oh wait, do that again. Death might be preferable to being your prisoner."

He opened the stall door and ushered her in before shutting it again. A large white mare Brea didn't recognize stood at the back. "You're not my prisoner."

"Oh really? Then what would you call forced marriage?"

"The deal you made."

"Only because I wanted Neeve released with Myles. I don't want to be your wife, Griffin. Sorry if that hurts your massive ego."

Pain flashed across his face, but it was gone as quickly as it appeared. "Contrary to what you believe, I don't want a wife who hates me. But neither of us have any choice, Brea. All we can do is live with this."

"If that's all you have to say, I have a ceiling to go stare at." She put a hand on the stall door, but Griff's voice held her back.

"Myles got away."

"What?" She twisted to face him once again. "Explain."

"On the way to the cottage, he and Neeve escaped the soldiers guarding them."

Brea slumped against the wall. "You mean Myles is out wandering Fargelsi?" This kingdom was dangerous, deadly. Myles may have been better off as a prisoner.

Griff gripped her shoulders and dipped his head to peer into her face. "He's okay."

"You don't know that."

"I do, actually. Brea, look at me."

She sniffed and lifted her eyes to his.

"He reached the border where the Eldurian scouts found him and Neeve and took them back to camp."

Her breath came in short gasps. "Eldur has them?" Relief flooded through her, but she didn't know if she could trust any of his words. "But how did they get across the border?"

He released her. "Call it an early wedding present."

"You..." She pushed out a breath. "You did this? You opened the border for them?"

"I placed one of my men among their guards. He had orders to look the other way. Regan never would have let you visit them, Brea. The cottage... it wouldn't be much better than the dungeons. I hate myself for abducting that boy from the human world and dragging him into this. I was only following orders, but maybe this helps make it right."

"Why do you do the awful things you do, Griff?"

Griff peeked out of the stall, eyeing the stable boys shoveling hay into barrels and feeding horses. None of them were close enough to hear. "I have to."

"But you don't."

"There are things you do not understand."

"Then explain them to me."

"I can't." He paused. "I came to her when I was two years old, Brea. I love Fargelsi. For all her faults, Regan raised me. She protected me and wants to make me her heir. I'm going to be the king of Fargelsi. And when that day comes, everything will change."

Brea sighed. "Power attracts the corruptible. Suspect any who seek it." If anyone asked her how she remembered that quote, she wouldn't know. Myles went through a Dune phase and repeated basically anything Frank Herbet ever said in his life. But those words had never seemed truer than in this moment as she stared at a man who could have been good. Griffin O'Shea was sweet and kind and noble.

But he wanted to be king, and that was where each one of those traits ended. He wasn't entitled to a crown or becoming heir for the good of the people. Regan convinced him it would make his life worthy.

"Brea—"

She cut him off with a look. "I'm sad for myself, Griff, but mostly I'm just sad for you." Now that Myles and Never were out of harm's way, it no longer mattered what happened to her.

"We have no choice in any of this." He leaned close, dropping his voice. "Brea, we have to make your aunt believe in our happy union."

Brea nodded. He was right. Regan had to think she'd gotten her way--which she had.

And then one day, Brea would get hers.

"Okay, where do we start?"

"A betrothal ceremony."

"Where are those triplets when you need them?" Brea grumbled as she pulled her hair free of the braid she'd been trying to wrap around the crown of her head. For most of her life, she'd thrown her hair into a ponytail and called it a day, but that didn't cut it in this fancy-pants world.

"Ugh!" She launched her jeweled comb across the room, and it flew out the door, landing with a crack in the hall.

Brea turned in her seat to find a slender woman standing in the doorway. Her blond hair was pulled back into a low braid worn by many of the servants. A green woolen dress hung off her too-skinny frame like a sack.

"Hello." Brea eyed the scared girl, realizing she knew her.

"It's you." Brea stood, her mouth hanging open. The last time she'd see her was years ago in the human world. She'd met her at a coffee shop and they'd really hit it off and spent the day together. Brea remembered falling asleep watching Netflix with her, but when she woke up the girl was gone and Brea was convinced it was all a hallucination. She'd forgotten all about that day until she laid eyes on her now. But she couldn't remember her name.

"I remem—"

"Hello, my Lady," she interrupted, dipping into a curtsy.

"I thought I made you up." Brea rushed across the room to hug her, but something in the girl's eyes reminded her they weren't alone.

"I have been sent to assist you, my Lady."

"Oh." Brea stopped short, her eyes scanning the room for any sign that Regan was listening. "Thank heavens you're here. I am completely hopeless with these whacked out fae hair styles."

The maid smiled, but there was something wrong behind it, something broken. Gone was the feisty girl Brea had once hoped to call friend.

The maid turned into the hall and picked up the comb with delicate fingers. Not saying a word, she walked toward Brea and began dragging the comb through her hair.

"Are you my new maid?" Brea stared at her in the looking glass.

"Yes, Lady Brea. The queen would like me to attend you from now on."

Brea almost smiled. Her aunt knew how much the triplets bothered her. But Regan didn't do anything for no reason.

"Please, just call me Brea."

The girl nodded as her deft hands wound Brea's hair into an intricate design over the crown of her head. By the time she was done, Brea was speechless. "How did you--"

Not even Neeve or Rowena would have been able to accomplish such a feat.

"I grew up in a fae court, my Lady." The girl walked toward the white dress that lay spread out on the end of the bed. "We must get you dressed for the ceremony."

Brea stood. "Are you going to tell me your name?" She wracked her brain, trying to remember the girl's name she met years ago.

"That has been forbidden." Her eyes tightened. "You must speak to me as little as possible."

"But why?"

"Please, let's get you dressed."

"I can get myself dressed. I'd like to know your name, please."

A knock sounded on the door, and Brea yanked it open before the maid could. Griff peered past her into the room with a grim expression. "I was in the hall and heard yelling."

"I wasn't yelling, and shouldn't you be getting ready for the ceremony?" Brea didn't have any more energy to hate him.

His eyes never left the maid as he wrapped an arm around Brea's back and pulled her close.

She pushed at his chest before remembering what he said about pretending. If she had to shove Lochlan from her mind and play love with Griff to stay alive, she could. This was a dangerous game, and the only way she could win was if she managed to keep her life.

Relaxing into him, she hugged him back.

"I can't wait to make you my fiancé today," Griff said, his voice loud for anyone listening in. Bringing his lips to her ear, he whispered. "Any secret you make your maid confess will cost her. Do not ask her questions."

"Why? What's going on, Griff?"

He released her and stepped back. "I must prepare myself." He put a hand on the door to close it behind him and stopped, turning to face her one last time. His lips formed a single, silent word. One that changed everything.

Alona.

The girl Regan sent to wait on Brea was the missing Eldurian princess, the human raised as fae. The one who had come to visit her in the human world when they were sixteen years old.

Brea turned to stare at her, knowing she'd been living her life for the last few months.

But not anymore. As their eyes met, understanding passed between them. Because they'd been in this together since the moment one baby was exchanged for another.

A betrothal ceremony had no real meaning other than a promise—ironic considering all of Griff's broken promises.

There would be no magic binding them together until they were truly wed, but now the people of the three kingdoms would know their intent. Over the next months citizens would trickle into Fargelsi to witness the Iskalt prince marrying the Fargelsian princess. It was a union blessed, and one Regan claimed was unbreakable.

She was probably right.

As Brea stood beside the doors to the garden where the ceremony would take place, she knew there was no going back. She'd made her choice, and it was time to live with it.

Cracks spidered through her heart as she pictured a different O'Shea brother waiting for her among the flowering trees and vine-covered benches. Lochlan would have hated every moment of this elaborate gathering.

Griff reveled in it.

Two brothers, so different in many ways, yet both stubborn and arrogant in the way of princes.

Alona stood behind Brea, a single ally in a sea of enemies. No others crowded the small space. Brea dropped her voice and turned to Alona. "I tried to free you too."

Alona's expression didn't change. She was resigned to her fate, and it broke Brea a little more. "Finn wanted me to tell you you're in his thoughts."

Tears welled in her eyes, and she blinked them away. "I wish he'd forget about me completely."

"He loves you."

Alona glanced behind them. "We must not speak of such things, Brea. Not ever."

Brea was about to argue when the heavy garden doors swung open, her cue to enter. No music played as she walked through the gardens, reminding her that this was not a wedding.

She reached the large oak tree shielding Griff from the sun. His auburn hair was combed back away from his face, revealing smooth, clean-shaved skin and sparkling eyes.

His smile lit up his entire face when he saw her, but all she could manage was a nervous twitch of her lips.

Regan stood next to Griff, her beaming smile a contradiction to her duplicitous nature.

No crowds awaited them, only the queen and a single maid. Brea searched for others before her aunt drew her attention.

"The kingdom will bless your marriage with extravagant parties, Brea. But a betrothal is for the earth, the very ground we walk on. Fargelsi receives its magic as a blessing from the land. It is now time for the land to bless your union as well. Come here." She held out a hand, and Brea took it, wondering how she'd once felt comfort in her aunt's touch.

Regan pulled her to stand in front of Griff, and as Brea gazed into his eyes, her heart pounded against her ribs. Because this wasn't right. It wasn't fair or just. People like Regan couldn't win. Guys like Griff shouldn't get the girl.

She wanted so desperately for it to be someone else standing in front of her. Tears built in her eyes as Regan began the blessing. When Griff clasped their hands together, the tears spilled down Brea's cheeks.

Regan wound a lacy bolt of silk over their hands, and Brea couldn't breathe.

For Myles, she told herself. She did this for her best friend, and she'd do it again. But that didn't stop the pain ripping through her heart or the hatred seething in her mind.

Griff acted as if he didn't notice her tears, as if they were the happy tears of a hopeful bride-to-be. His denial would never change the outcome. A part of her would always hate him for not being Lochlan O'Shea.

As Regan finished the blessing, all Brea could think of was that she shouldn't be here. She belonged by Lochlan's side, fighting with the army she'd helped assemble.

Instead, she was a puppet, a pawn.

She met Alona's sad eyes, and it took everything she had to keep from falling to the stone pathway in a garden that wasn't hers. Her garden, her courtyard had a naked man fountain and coins representing every wish she'd tried to force into being.

Now, she had nowhere to put her wishes.

She stumbled back to her room to change before going to the main hall for the lunch celebrating the betrothal. As she crossed the threshold into her room, her legs gave out beneath her, and she fell to the floor, not feeling the impact.

Sobs wracked her body, and Alona's arms came around her, keeping her from collapsing onto her side and curling into a ball like she wanted to do.

"Shhh," Alona whispered. Maybe she was reminding her

they were being listened to, or maybe it was just comfort, but Brea didn't want to be quiet. She wanted to rage against Fargelsi and rebel against her aunt. She wanted to ride into battle with the Eldur crest on her chest.

And most of all, she wanted to see Lochlan again. Just once.

They'd had no news out of Iskalt, but he had to be alive. This world wouldn't be right without Lochlan O'Shea barking orders and being his general douchey self.

She wouldn't be right.

"I love him," she whispered as more tears clogged her throat.

"Me too," Alona answered.

They were speaking of different men they might never see again, but in that, they were together.

Two girls trapped in a foreign palace with no light to guide them home.

The plan was doomed from the start.

Lure the Iskalt soldiers from the castle into a fight. Sounded simple. The miscalculation? It took them two days to leave the safety of their high walls, two days for Lochlan to taunt his uncle.

Now Callum wanted him dead.

"Retreat!" he yelled. "Everyone, fall back!" He kicked his horse around and thundered into the valley beyond the Iskalt palace. "Retreat!"

The Iskalt citizens who'd joined his side followed the command as they used their magic to combat that of the people behind them.

The sun rose on the horizon, and with each passing moment, Lochlan's magic faded like the stars in the sky.

Pain ripped up his leg as an arrow struck him, and he

screamed. His horse reared back before picking up speed. Another arrow sailed toward him, and he yanked on the reins. The horse threw him from his back and kept running.

Lochlan stumbled to his feet and stared down at the arrow shaft lodged in his thigh. Grabbing it with two hands, he broke it, leaving the head still in his leg. There would be time to remove it later.

Dizziness overcame him for just a moment as horses galloped past him followed by foot soldiers. He joined the steady stream of Iskalt warriors fighting against his uncle. They had to make it over the next hill before Callum's men caught up with them.

This was where the plan was doomed.

As the dawn came, Iskalt magic lessened, but they had a force of Eldur soldiers Callum knew nothing about.

If they made it to them.

Lochlan hadn't counted on the size of Callum's force tripling his. He didn't think it would take this long to goad his uncle into a real battle. Callum was rash, not one to abide a siege.

But battles over open ground—those he reveled in.

And now he'd have one.

Lochlan held his sword tightly as he ran, even as the strength in his hands lessened. He could see their destination on the other side of the valley, a hill of snow and ice, behind which the Eldurian forces hid.

Pain enveloped him with every step he took, but he couldn't stop now, not when so many people were counting on him.

The only thing that kept him moving was picturing Brea in his mind. A messenger from Finn told him they had Myles and Brea's friend, Neeve. She'd done it. She'd saved her friends. But what was happening to her now?

The only way to save her was to win this fight, this crown, and take his kingdom back. Only then could Iskalt and Eldur march on Fargelsi. Only then could they stop the pain and strife throwing their world into human-like chaos.

And it started here, with this pain he overcame every time his boot hit the snow.

Every time he wobbled and didn't fall.

Every time he saw his people risk their lives for their kingdom.

Being king wasn't about power or luxury. He only wanted to do what was right.

His strength waned as he crested the final hill among the thundering horses and Iskaltians running for their lives.

But with the dawn came a new strength. As his power and that of his people faded away, the Eldurians' power grew.

And they were ready.

By the time Callum's men pounded over the hill to find fresh troops full of fire magic awaiting them, it was too late.

A new day had dawned in Iskalt.

And with it came a man who was finally worthy of wearing the crown.

Want more from Brea's world?

Don't miss the free prequel,
Fae's Dilemma available at

https://www.subscribepage.com/faesdilemmanovella

And look for your FREE bonus chapters
available at the end of Fae's Destruction:
Queens of the Fae Book 3

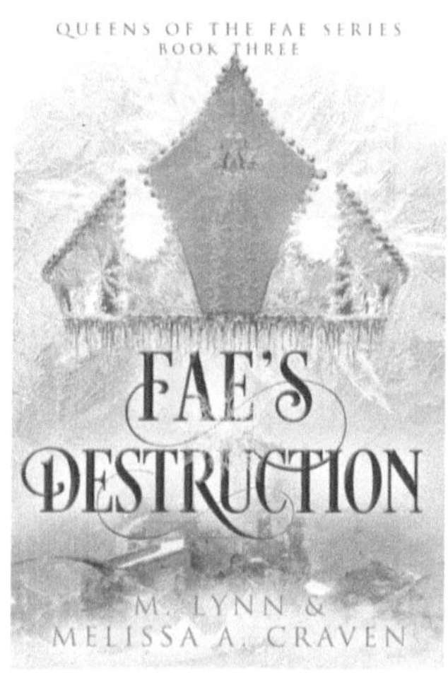

Brea Robinson is a prisoner.

Granted, her prison has gilded halls, servants, and an aunt intent on throwing a lavish wedding. A wedding for Brea. Fae marriages are unbreakable, everlasting.

As Brea barrels toward her forever prison in a marriage to a man she doesn't love, the three Fae kingdoms are thrown into turmoil. But no matter how close Queen Regan's enemies get, it won't be enough to save Brea from the fate she chose.

Some sacrifices result in death. Others only make you wish for death.

Brea didn't surrender herself to the powerful Fargelsi Queen for nothing. She saved her best friend and found the missing princess. She said goodbye to the man she loved so he could reclaim his throne.

Everything has a purpose, everyone has a role to play and if marrying the wrong brother is hers, at least she'll help bring an end to this war.

Because Queen Regan O'Rourke might be family, but her rule is over.

It's time for a new generation to unite the Fae.

ABOUT MELISSA A. CRAVEN

Melissa A. Craven writes YA Contemporary and YA Fantasy (Contemporary fans will know her as Ann Maree Craven). Her books feature strong female protagonists who aren't always perfect, but find their inner strength along the way. Melissa believes in stories that make you think and she loves foreshadowing, leaving clues and hints for the careful reader.

Melissa draws inspiration from her background in architecture and interior design to help her with the small details in world building and scene settings. She is a diehard introvert with a wicked sense of humor and a tendency for hermit-like behavior. (She gets cranky if she has to put on anything other than yoga pants and t-shirts!)

Visit Melissa at Melissaacraven.com for more information about her newest series and discover exclusive content.

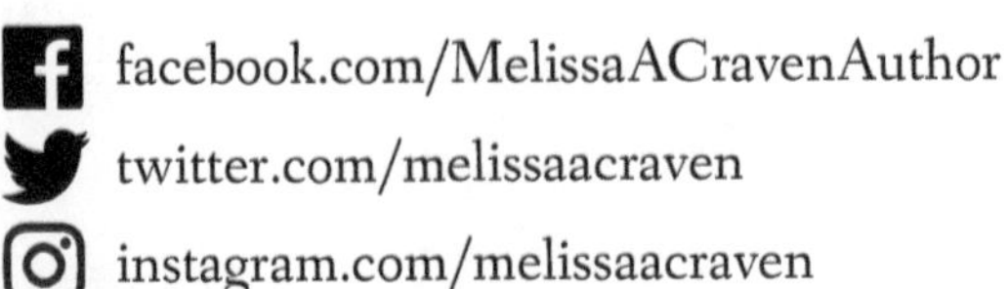

ALSO BY MELISSA A. CRAVEN

QUEENS OF THE FAE

Fae's Deception | *Fae's Defiance* | *Fae's Destruction*

CRIMES OF THE FAE

Fae's Prisoner | *Fae's Power* | *Fae's Promise*

IMMORTALS OF INDRIELL

Emerge (Book 1) | *Edge (Book 0)* | *Catalyst (Short Story)*

Judgment (Book 2) | *Scholar (Series Companion)* |

Volunteer (Short Story) | *Captive (Book 3)*

Assignment (Novella) | *Heir (Book 4)* | *Betrayal (Book 5)*

Runaway (Book 6) Coming soon | *Proving (Book 7) Coming Soon*

ASCENSION OF THE NINE REALMS

(Coming Soon)

Valkyrie | *Warder* | *Berserker* | *Druid*

ABOUT M. LYNN

Michelle MacQueen is a USA Today bestselling author of love. Yes, love. Whether it be YA romance, NA romance, or fantasy romance (Under M. Lynn), she loves to make readers swoon.

The great loves of her life to this point are two tiny blond creatures who call her "aunt" and proclaim her books to be "boring books" for their lack of pictures. Yet, somehow, she still manages to love them more than chocolate.

When she's not sharing her inexhaustible wisdom with her niece and nephew, Michelle is usually lounging in her ridiculously large bean bag chair creating worlds and characters that remind her to smile every day - even when a feisty five-year-old is telling her just how much she doesn't know.

See more from Michelle MacQueen and sign up to receive updates and deals!

www.michellelynnauthor.com

ALSO BY M. LYNN

QUEENS OF THE FAE

Fae's Deception | *Fae's Defiance* | *Fae's Destruction*

CRIMES OF THE FAE

Fae's Prisoner | *Fae's Power* | *Fae's Promise*

THE HIDDEN WARRIOR

Dragon Rising | *Dragon Rebellion*

FANTASY AND FAIRYTALES

Golden Curse | *Golden Chains* | *Golden Crown*

Glass Kingdom | *Glass Princess*

Noble Thief | *Cursed Beauty*

LEGACY OF LIGHT

A War For Magic | *A War For Truth* | *A War For Love*

A War For Love

www.ingramcontent.com/pod-product-compliance
Lightning Source LLC
Chambersburg PA
CBHW030527310726
48979CB00010B/1834/J

9781970052107